NO DEAL

BERTIL DUNÉR

The Book Guild Ltd

First published in Great Britain in 2021 by
The Book Guild Ltd
9 Priory Business Park
Wistow Road, Kibworth
Leicestershire, LE8 0RX
Freephone: 0800 999 2982
www.bookguild.co.uk
Email: info@bookguild.co.uk
Twitter: @bookguild

Copyright © 2021 Bertil Dunér

The right of Bertil Dunér to be identified as the author of this
work has been asserted by him in accordance with the
Copyright, Design and Patents Act 1988.

All rights reserved. No part of this publication may be
reproduced, transmitted, or stored in a retrieval system, in any form or by any means,
without permission in writing from the publisher, nor be otherwise circulated in
any form of binding or cover other than that in which it is published and without
a similar condition being imposed on the subsequent purchaser.

This work is entirely fictitious and bears no resemblance to any persons living or dead.

Typeset in 11pt minion pro

Printed on FSC accredited paper
Printed and bound in Great Britain by 4edge Limited

ISBN 978 1913551 667

British Library Cataloguing in Publication Data.
A catalogue record for this book is available from the British Library.

To Solveig
and Svea

PART I

1

Normally, I wouldn't have opened the letter, but it stuck out from the middle of the stack; and then there was the stamp. A wide foaming waterfall, lush riverbanks, dark-trunked trees leaning recklessly out over the edge. Could be from the southeast. Falling for a nice stamp is no worse than being seduced by a pretty wine label, can happen to anybody.

> Dear Mr Birger
> Do you know this poem? I learned it by heart as a schoolgirl and have tried to make the best of it all my life.
> *I shall be telling this with a sigh*
> *Somewhere ages and ages hence:*
> *Two roads diverged in a wood, and I—*
> *I took the one less travelled by,*
> *And that has made all the difference.*

Oh, what a beginning. Eye-catching, though.

> Please note that I am not writing this letter of my own volition but because my hand is being forced; and as you may understand, we must clutch at straws.

One page, borders dotted with tiny hearts, tightly written, no photo or anything; I fancied she was a teacher. At the bottom of the page, there was a postscript:

I have been to your Madan Mogra orphanage, which is a shining example to all of us. Alas, out of reach. One of the girls has made such a nice sketch of you! It would be uplifting beyond words for us if you would let me meet you there sometime.

My wife believes that my sensitivity, or whimsicality, makes me ill-equipped to handle this kind of letter. Nothing wrong with my faculties, though; any residual deficiency is kept at bay with just two tiny blue pills.

My task is to go by the hotel on one of my daily strolls to pick up our mail. Madeleine attends to these letters; she classifies them into three categories, then acts on them. I contrived these categories myself but the implementation is uniquely her business. Most of them land in category one (the recycling box), she says; perhaps not this waterfall one.

Really awkward things are category three; some are even three plus, in which case they are forwarded to Jens in Copenhagen, when he isn't having a stint in Portugal or Geneva. While such letters were few and far between a year ago, they have become more frequent since the '*Wonder Turk*' article appeared in the *Bombay Times* last autumn, and was subsequently reprinted elsewhere in India and around the world.

Jens is my second self, if not to say my first self in many matters – managing all the undertakings I have a hand in, and then besides, I sometimes outsource tricky moral things to him or at least get his opinion about them.

2

It was only a few days after this Waterfall Letter that Carlos arrived, and almost despite myself, I wondered whether he was coming with his hand out. Why not? He may have come across *Wonder Turk* somewhere – an article, by the way, which was full of exaggeration in whole and in part.

Wandering into our kitchen, there was nothing self-conscious about him. He had given no notice other than adding in the tiniest handwriting in one of his monthly postcards, two dozen in all, that he might get a chance to come by some day.

Fairly tanned and wearing black-rimmed glasses, he was otherwise the same apple-cheeked young man, I thought, keeping his distance as ever, though perhaps with a firmer gaze. He may have found us about the same too; some more loose skin, perhaps, a bit of knee stiffness – fairly acceptable ravages of time so far, not much to make a fuss about.

Madeleine and Carlos embraced enthusiastically; at least Madeleine did, and sprinkled him with eager questions. Where did you land, Izmir or Antalya? Are you short-sighted or long-sighted? Are you hungry? Is that all your baggage?

I was quite content to be just a listener, and besides, I was on the phone finding out if there was a chance of being served slow roasted lamb somewhere, which would be a nice treat for someone who had been to both Australia and New Zealand.

Madeleine asked:

"How long are you staying?"

"Oh, that depends… We'll come back to that later, okay?"

It didn't take him long to make a tour of the house, and he evidently found no reason to linger anywhere. Coming to my workroom on the second floor, he said: "You have an office elsewhere, right?"

"No, I haven't." I shook my head.

"Oh, really?"

He pushed at his glasses with his right index finger. Quite naturally assuming I was somehow engaged in managing, he said, "But as an owner, I fancy you must maintain close contacts?"

This was not the moment to explain my situation in full, so I just said that I was invited to walk into a boardroom several times a year. But I didn't care to tell him I was free to turn down these invites.

Our little hamlet is lucky to have a hotel of its own. If just two-starred, it has an elevated terrace as well as a pool and, what's more, a kitchen superior to anything you can find down at the shore. Now, slow roasted lamb was not within their reach on this occasion, but we were promised traditional Turkish shish kebab. Its location is also to its credit; it sits in a thin broadleaf grove at a favourable distance from the sea – a ten-minute walk across a bushy wasteland, unless you choose the longer path around it, an austere turnpike mostly for tourists, the tanning shoal, so to speak.

Zia had taken up his stand at the entrance, which in fact is a superfluous portico. Working or not working, he wears dark trousers – blue today – and a white shirt, which somehow gives him an elderly look. His age is difficult to tell, as you would have to make allowances for his smoking, and working under the sun has taken its toll too; for many years, he was involved in repairing pipelines in Kurdistan.

At the sight of us, he vanished for a moment, presumably to rouse the chef, before appearing again to shake hands profusely with all three of us, meaning also with Madeleine. It was past lunchtime and hours before dinner, and we were the only guests. He lit the infrared heaters on the terrace. Clouds hung over the mountain ridge as if contemplating in what way they would fall over us.

While chatting with Zia, who I regard as a personal friend as much as a hotel employee, it emerged that he had already met Carlos down at the grocery store, and had shown him in the sand how to find his way to our house. Now, on hearing that Carlos was far from an ordinary visitor, Zia's everyday face, gloomy with furrows on either side of his nose, brightened and triggered a futile flash of wit on my part in recounting the parable of the Lost Son. It just discombobulated him, probably because there is no such thing as the Lost Son in the Quran, not that he is a follower of Islam, far from it. Anyway, Zia must have thought Carlos was a Golden Boy and so grew more and more curious to know in what way. "Carlos just got back from travelling the world," I said, "three years," and putting three fingers in the air, I pulled the plug on it. Soon enough, Zia started to hang red and white bunting around us, from on top of the gliding terrace doors to the beams of the corrugated plastic roof.

For dessert, he brought ice cream; generous portions decorated with the Turkish flag and an umbrella side by side that he put down in front of Madeleine and me. We hadn't ordered ice cream; we certainly didn't grumble. It is made from local fruits and berries and is a firm favourite. But why only two bowls when we had seen him carrying twice as many countless times without problems?

Presently, he entered again, gracefully, with a tray in his hands, on which sat an enormous ice cream crowned by a lit sparkler with a crowd of little red flags and umbrellas around it.

Carlos pulled out one of the flags, stood up and raised it urbanely towards the ceiling: "Thank you, *teşekkürler*, thank you," he said in a merry voice, and Zia made a bow to us all.

His circumnavigation may have made a different man of him, I thought, to the extent that a man can change at all, that is.

3

When I first laid eyes on Carlos, he was not much more than a toddler.

It so happened that I needed physiotherapy for tension headache, what with my work and everything else, and Madeleine became my therapist. Her sweet-smelling hands gave me temple and shoulder massages and I was given homework assignments – relaxation and meditation exercises.

After a couple of sessions, I thought I could identify her hand cream – yes, hydrocortisone 1% – and no wonder; as a dermatologist, it is a rather common cream for eczema. I had never particularly appreciated its scent before as I did then.

It came into my head, once therapy was over after ten sessions, to call on her at home. I chanced that she was single and would tackle it this way: if there was a man with her I would just say hallo and thanks again for everything you did for me, I´m much better now. If not, I would tell her I had something to show her. I would buy some health appliance or other from a healthcare shop to bring along in a big sports bag. As it happened, I opted for an orthopaedic buckwheat pillow. Or possibly an automatic massage mat, I don't remember.

Depression entrepreneurialism at its best; I must have been quite ready to accept her seeing through it on the spot.

I pressed the doorbell twice without anything happening on

the other side of the frosted window. Then there was a slight fumbling with the door handle, and after some moments, I decided to give it a push from my side. That's how I met Carlos.

He challenged me to wrestle with him on the spot, still too young to pronounce the word correctly. Dressed in Pippi Longstocking tights, one leg orange, the other green, but no shirt, he led me to a large playmat next to the TV covered with toys that he enthusiastically whisked away with his bare feet.

Even though I was kneeling, he was still some distance shorter than me. Screaming wildly, he threw himself at me, and however much I grappled and grunted he got me down on my back within minutes and crowned his victory by giving the V sign with both hands and shouting for his mother.

We got along well. Not just our wrestling at every visit; there was also my reading *Three Little Pigs, The Ugly Duckling* and telling him stories that popped up from within me, mostly about *Mr and Mrs Bubblegum*, who because of their chewing spoke only *bubblegumish*, had invented their own sign language and competed over who could put the most bubblegum in their mouths and still say, "I like bubblegum like an alligator." I genuinely enjoyed it all but its basis was of course my designs on Madeleine. As it was, over the course of a few months, I gradually moved in with them.

Carlos' early childhood was fairly regular; neither good nor bad at school, slightly above average, classmates and pals okay, a member of a football team. As his teenage years drew near, things changed, as was not completely unexpected perhaps. He had already had a basic laptop for a few years when he suddenly wanted something much better: a gaming computer, *High End!* Soon he wasn't alive to much beyond this new, formidable partner. Spirited away, even to the degree of stridently asserting his right to eat dinner while on it. Not allowed to, though.

He clearly had deft fingers, but was less quick on foot; we no longer saw him playing football. He neglected his schoolwork too, more and more, and we started to get worried. The difference between us was whether Carlos was like something akin to the founder of Facebook or someone like that – freaks, deplorable people, whether making money hand over fist or not. Madeleine's misgivings had a four-letter something, my suspicion.

If we couldn't work on him, maybe the school psychologist could? We requested a meeting and, much to our surprise, Carlos agreed to come with us and put up with it for three-quarters of an hour. The psychologist – Henry, a former psychiatrist wearing jeans, whereas for my part I had thought it appropriate to change – took pains to calm us down. Even if there were anything amiss with Carlos, he couldn't be labelled ADHD.

"He is certainly not an average kid, but still on the normal side."

Out of pure relief, I blurted out: "Why normal, when the boy is suffering from chronic htpp and HTML?"

Henry was on board: "Yes, and WWW! But that's not really deviant behaviour, not any longer," he added, faintly smiling, "just a matter of different lifestyle."

On leaving, we shook hands with Henry. Carlos too, who if anything looked quite content. That they had often been chatting with each other when Henry was on yard duty was something we only learned later.

4

Carlos was left to himself.

It was nice to see his new, active persona at close quarters. That he had been away for such a long time without any distress calls or anything, and was apparently not penniless, was more than we could have hoped for.

On foot, by bus or in a taxi, which he apparently preferred to using our car, which was 'too cramped', he went sightseeing all over until two suitcases arrived and the tours became longer and extended over several days. He swapped Capri pants and t-shirts for a thin flannel suit, and carried a video camera and a laptop in a shoulder bag. With his own eyes, he could see, and document it too if he wanted, that Turkey's south coast was rapidly developing; counting the cranes when he visited Antalya, he got bored when he reached fifty. "I've seen everything from Bodrum to Side," he said. Not until later did I understand it wasn't just sightseeing.

"Kash is a nice place," he said. "I want to go back there someday to swim with the dolphins." In fact, this was one of the few opportunities for us to do something together.

Turks are not very good at English, he established. Anyway, it's cool to listen to their own language even though it's just abracadabra.

He asked me, "Are you fluent in Turkish?"

"Well, I'm working on it. Not full proficiency yet."

"Is it worth it?"

"I don't know, never given it a thought. Learning a language is its own reward if you ask me."

"What about around here?" he asked. "Not much moving, eh?"

Did he mean in the village itself, or here in this coastal community?

"Here, let's say. Those two skeletons, hotels or whatever, will never be finished, I've been told."

"The politicians in the village have promised to plant poplars around them, which is something at least," I said jokingly. "But there are two more houses recently built in our row. Ten now. Pretty nice places for *gecekondus*."

"What's that?"

"*Put up at night*, without building permits, rumour has it," I say with a chuckle. "Too many of them, perhaps. Rumours, I mean."

I felt I should try to come up with more. Just outside the village, round the corner from the derelict Turkish bath, there will be a petrol station soon; at least site preparation has been done. Otherwise, I say with mock pride, our hotel has just got a brass nameplate, on a chain hanging from a pole and twinkling in the sun in recognition of me when I come to pick up our mail. "Not a big thing for mankind, but big enough for me," I add.

Carlos of course was not even born when Neil Armstrong set his foot in the dust of the moon.

*

"I have been earning my bread, as you know, but I have been studying too," Carlos says, rather unexpectedly. "I'm about to pocket an MBA in a matter of weeks."

Madeleine is ironing, one of her favourite occupations. She puts down the iron with a crash.

"Oh, Carlos, how nice!" She is beaming and would have gone to give him a hug if the worn cord hadn't got tangled up.

"MBA," I drawl gaily, "sounds like… *Meditation* something. Or *Mindful*?"

My guesses don't visibly change anything in his face; but whatever his look held, it wasn't pleasure. Just before setting out on his gap-year odyssey, we had found some common ground, albeit a bit frost-bound. It still was, apparently, and our idiosyncrasies don't match.

"*Master of Business Administration*," he replies tersely.

I hasten to say: "Oh my! Tell us all about it!"

He might have thought me facetious. All right, but only up to a point because there was also genuine ignorance in there too. Company owner though I am, the acronym was unknown to me. And my therapy associations came naturally as mindful meditation is something I have tried, and is also, by the way, an anti-stress method Madeleine sometimes teaches at Turkish retreat hotels.

"This is the type of MBA that requires a thesis."

I ask what about, but he shakes his head: It isn't something that can be explained straight off.

"Please try," exhorts Madeleine.

In the living room, where we have our evenings at home, the door into the garden was open to let in the afternoon rustle from under the fig bushes; hedgehogs and quails, we believe. Madeleine resumed her work, but turned the ironing board a little to get a better view of Carlos.

"It's a complex set of issues," he says, "that three of us graduates are tackling from the point of view of the potential change of management skills that are needed in the new international environment following the credit crisis of 2008."

I was seated in the shorter of the two sofas, opposite Carlos, slightly bowing forward, presumably, as I tend to do when there is something that demands my full concentration.

"The traditional paradigm for executive skills is skewed – excessive use of quantitative methods, and so on, and, more importantly, neglect of the nature of human capacity."

My eyes were fixed on the centre of the parquet table between us, exactly where the walnut strips make up a cross, as if the meaning of his project were somehow latent there. I refrained from glancing at Madeleine, although it appeared that her ironing had slowed down somewhat. As with knitting, ironing is something restful for her, and she loves the smell of steam penetrating newly washed cotton (mostly physiotherapy uniforms) – easily overtaking the wafts of lavender from the large flower pot just outside the terrace door.

"Dear Carlos, can you rephrase it for me?" she said. "My brain is too small for this."

She went too far, if you ask me, no need to excuse oneself for being unfamiliar with abstractitis.

"All right." He drew a breath. "The world of finance, which will have to be led by MBAs, is slow to see crises coming and inept at handling them. Just think of the euro crisis." It was almost you felt as if he was exerting himself, like a dog trainer shouting *heel*, with the puppy searching Master's eyes, head uplifted.

"So MBA programmes for potential leaders have to be radically modified."

Now he turned towards me: "The medical profession has the same problem, don't you think? It's not enough to teach doctors which pills to prescribe. They must have human qualities; *consultation competence* if you like."

"Aha," I said, seizing the opportunity to agree with him.

"The quality of potential business leaders is different

of course. We should trace their *human fitness* as early as possible, and primarily for those that companies send on MBA programmes."

"So it's panning out the human nuggets among MBA students?"

"Yes, as a component of the admissions process. I have given this a great deal of thought. It is basically a matter of finding *indicators*."

"Indicators? How do you mean?"

"Take *fever*. If a patient has a fever, this is an indicator that there is something amiss, right? So among those that businesses want to invest in, it would be a good thing to find those with a fever, as a way of putting it."

"I see the parallel. But knowing about someone's fever isn't very helpful in itself. It may originate from anything from sunstroke to pneumonia or rheumatism, or an innocent virus."

"A good point," he said, making a twisting left-hand movement. "That's why we must come up with several indicators, just as doctors have fever, sedimentation rate, blood tests, and more, to hand."

I didn't know what to make of it all, feeling rubbed up the wrong way. I kept my counsel, though, as I still had my facetious lapse to atone for.

"Have you yourself been scrutinised in this way?" I asked mildly.

"No! There is no such thing yet!"

He smiled, even gave a chuckle. "And that's what makes this idea so great, so challenging. We are three people working on it, as I said, each writing his thesis on it."

That much Carlos had said before dinner in the village to celebrate the good news. We drank fine Turkish red wine – even I, after first having taken some antacids. In my student years in

Sweden, wine was sold only at government shops, and there was just one Turkish wine on the shelves, with the risible name of *Beyaz*, meaning white. Bad, very bad, but far cheaper than the rest, and for that reason alone, very popular with us medical students. Here, in Turkey, it has dawned on us that good wines are also produced, fine enough, as I later learned from a well-known wine guru, to win international awards.

On finishing the second bottle of *Oküzgözü* (Bull's eye), Carlos had some parting words:

"You see, if a business company sends a rising star to get an MBA without him being tested along our lines, they run the risk of coming up with a Mediocre Business Ass."

Rather amazed, I found this even rawer than anything my facetiousness had been able to come up with. I joined him in a hearty laugh.

5

Whenever I feel the need to walk off some unruly thoughts, I go down to the corner where the beach ends and the southern promontory juts out into the sea, then follow a path which slowly meanders upwards between pine trees and loose boulders, revealing an increasingly beautiful view of the blue sea and the undulating interior with tightly scattered greenhouses like pale spangles on a folded skirt of many-hued green.

The village stands out clearly from five miles away, the slender minaret rising over the rooftops. From this mountainside, you can hear the calls to prayer (including the throat clearings, always at the same place) much more distinctly than anywhere else in our Liman community. I wonder how many attend the mosque. This is not a prosperous village, quite the contrary, but no toothless jaws, though.

Every so often, I looked out into the bay. This was the time of the year when people were beginning to come down to the sand, but more chairs were still piled up than not.

I could see two people perched on the edge of the elevated jetty, their backs to the sun and to me too. Half way out, a man was sitting with the lower part of his legs hanging down, and something shining at his side, his shoes too. Wide back.

It occurred to me that it could well be Carlos.

He had been up early that morning to send a disc to Melbourne; that's the only way they accept a longer document. And now he was sitting there with his computer? But his thesis was finished, wasn't it? As Carlos is probably just as sensitive to a feeling of being controlled now as he was when younger, I hadn't asked him about it.

There was a woman sitting there too, a bit on the dark side, slim, wearing a wine-red, sleeveless blouse, something yellow below. An ornament in her hair, or flowers. Seemingly, they were not talking to each other. I could spy on them at leisure if I wanted, which I did, while telling myself that at bottom I wasn't curious at all.

What roused my attention was the distance between them. Carlos was a little bit taller than I and, to the best of my knowledge, normally proportioned. And so, in line with this Leonardo drawing of the human body, what I saw of Carlos' back would be half his length, minus a reduction for not sitting erect. In other words, 90-odd centimetres. Now, the distance between the two appeared to be slightly more than two backs, making 2 metres more or less.

Had I still been a child of seven, I would have puffed at the Sherlock Holmes pipe that an uncle gave me as a birthday present: *What do you make of this, Watson? A rather devilish gap, isn't it? Are these two together or are they not? There is a third alternative, mark you: at least one of them has intentions towards the other.*

Enlivened by this distraction, I continued at increased pace up the slope but halted briefly at the next turn of the winding path. From this new angle, the big cliff in the middle of the bay appeared like a wedge of hard cheese nicely cut out from a huge wheel, still there at the next turn again but less harmonious in form, the more ill-shaped the higher up you go. A misty day would still leave it as a cheese wedge, but mouldy.

I couldn't hold back serial speculation. This girl could well be Zia's daughter, the eldest of three, who has some sort of job at the Teachers' Union Hostel a stone's throw away.

I wished I had been able to distinguish Carlos' facial features, to find out what they would be like when meeting a young woman that he was possibly chasing. He doesn't exert himself overly hard in our company, at least not in mine, to make himself agreeable. In a way, this suits me fine, in principle, as it keeps him natural, and keeps down the risk of obsequiousness, too.

Yet, his stolid mien…

No, no, I'm being unfair, there is nothing wrong with his face or even the shape of his mouth, not at all, only with the flimsy smile that goes with it most of the time, no more than an indication, rarely more than that, which might be taken for unconcern or, even worse, irony. No bed of roses at a tryst, I'm sure, or in the world of business.

*

That same day, in the afternoon, who should I run into in Kerim's grocery shop but Carlos' jetty seatmate – if Carlos it were, of course – and, yes, she was Zia's daughter all right; *Elif*, or *Chichek,* which was her pet name, meaning *Flower* – the eldest one who had grown considerably since I last saw her in the company of her father; he was riding his Yamaha with Chichek riding pillion behind, carrying his helmet. Indeed, she had turned into a woman. She must be nearly twenty now, even twenty-one or twenty-two?

Her yellow shorts were both tight and short – and, given that she in all likelihood lived under Zia's roof, I marvelled that he condoned it – beautifully matching her thighs, the colour of Nestlé cappuccino powder; such limbs as might prove an asset or a handicap, depending on how you look at it.

In spite of Kerim's shop being rather small, really only one aisle, there was no eye contact between us. Her shopping was not complicated, *ayran*, the Turkish yogurt beverage, and a couple of apples. Nor was mine: a chocolate bar and the *Milliet* newspaper with its *Aegean Supplement.* I could easily have overtaken her, making a detour which wouldn't have delayed me much on my way home to my new reading chair but, as it happened, I strode away decisively in the opposite direction, nobly bottling up my curiosity.

For all that, my speculations were not at an end. The jetty, I thought, wasn't a bad place for a tryst, if you wanted, located close to her place of work, with its middle part hidden from view from the beach road by a grove of leafy Indian pearl trees, in case she didn't want word spread about the budding dalliance.

The distance between them, neither near nor far, was funny. An extra security precaution? Nothing of this could be verified, of course, definitely not through Carlos. Unless he truly wanted you to know, you might as well try to get blood out of a stone.

6

For the ride to Kash, we rented a car with a driver, to make it really comfortable. It was a scenic drive along the Turquoise Coast, which we find far more captivating than either the French or the Italian Riviera and is far less developed, not least as the rugged mountains stubbornly raise objections.

Carlos, in the backseat of this black Mercedes together with Madeleine, is leaning forward to ask questions: many people in your companies with MBAs or similar diplomas?

I thought about it but couldn't lie.

"I have no idea."

"Really? How many companies do you have?"

Though I tried my best, or near to it, it was a jerky conversation, not without a certain irritation, I should think. Turning your neck for a long time is tiresome for many older people (it strains the *levator scapula*), and an ordeal for me.

"Yes, I have stakes in several companies, but honestly I'm not clear about the exact terms of ownership, which is complicated. No matter, really, as Jens, my Danish friend of many years standing –his family all friends of ours - is responsible for it all. Apart from the Madan Mogra. Did you know I'm supporting an orphanage in India? Without any claims; my interest is of a quite different kind, just a symbolic role left now, honorary chairman."

"Uh-huh," he says, and slowly withdraws his head from between the seats like a tortoise.

Then he is back, asking about Jens. "Well, Jens, that's a long story. I first met him at a conference in London, and later he took the initiative to exploit my discoveries. Your mother was helpful too."

Our chauffeur is a middle-aged man who runs a shuttle service to and from the airports and a few hotels in our area. A seasoned driver, he doesn't let others rush him and so is frequently overtaken, not least where road markings happen to forbid it, and at stop signs, and he breaks the car respectfully for goats and sheep by the roadside.

Occasionally glancing at him, I try to guess what he might be making of our talk; not that it matters, of course. A little perhaps. There are plenty of international loanwords in Turkish, *conference* for one, and he certainly knows who I am – well known to people in Liman, and far beyond.

At length, Carlos asks me: "How come you are not running your businesses? You are not too old for that, you know?"

"In fact, Jens wants me to be more than an absentee owner, an *eminence gris,* whereas I'm content to be less, a *grey hermite.* Yes, there is this tug of war."

I take a gulp of air and twist a little in my seat before continuing:

"In a way, it's all about taking decisions, the downsides."

"What's the problem, when you are the owner? I never thought of you as being afraid of conflict."

"Fair enough. In my earlier jobs, I often even sought it, like a terrier. To sort things out. I was a Moral Janitor, sweeping the corridors as often as I could."

"Really?"

"These days, it's more that I don't want to come into conflict with myself…"

Carlos wouldn't understand – and how could he? Fortunately, he didn't follow up on it. Then again, he must have had an idea about what had happened to me not so long ago. If nothing else, he must have heard details from Madeleine. Overworked; more than that, which I would be willing to broach when convenient, sometime when there was peace and quiet and nothing scheduled for the three of us. When an ordinary working day's hassles take on the proportions of an existential threat, it is really serious. So it had been for me.

The road meanders, several hairpin turns, now dropping down towards the water, now rising high up on the mountain. Our driver slowed when particularly beautiful vistas opened up before us.

Above the windscreen there was a picture of a woman with a child and also a homemade card: 'The most genuine *mürşit* in life is science'. I didn't know the word *mürşit*, so I couldn't make out the meaning. Most drivers put up something religious. Maybe it was *seducer*, and he was an intelligent-design man, an anti-creationist. There are lots of them in this country. Would it be rude to ask?

"*Mürşit* means seducer or something?"

"Oh no, it's *guide*, an old word."

"Aha," I say, feeling relieved. "Words of Atatürk?"

"Yep, Kemal Pasha," he replies, visibly pleased.

Minutes later, he brakes firmly and the car comes to a halt at the roadside under a rockfall fence on the red cliff face.

"I'll show you something quite unusual!"

Like a crowd of goats, we jump across the busy road over to the precipice. Two thin strips of sand far down there, but these are not what he has in mind for us. He makes a sweeping movement: "Have you ever seen so many shades of blue?"

Madeleine's eyes naturally bulge a little and now she has opened them wide. "Oh my! Azur and cyan," she says and begins to point. "Cobalt blue and that blue of old Chinese porcelain, aquamarine and, there, like our Japanese irises. And the September charms I had…"

"The ones we had in Sweden," I wondered. "Rather pink, those?"

"Yes, at first they were, then turning lilac."

Madeleine, as a young woman, had taken courses in watercolour at Skagen, but not even she had enough words to describe it all.

Her rapture was unmistakable and with her hands and facial expressions, she tried to convey it all to Carlos, who was slow to react: "You know, Australia and New Zealand may have left me a bit jaded, I guess."

"Beautiful, overpowering," I translate to the driver.

While dashing back to the car, he shouted:

"A bit dicey to stop here, but I thought you would appreciate it."

Not until we saw Kash sprawling below us, quite picturesque for a tourist town, was Carlos enthused. He pointed through the window. "The bluish island out there! That's Megisti. It's Greece, European Union, takes you less than fifteen minutes."

7

Carlos is being towed around the wide pool by a dolphin. I hadn't noticed his muscular frame before –newly acquired perhaps. Even in the water he wore his one-size-fits-all countenance, rather like a dolphin himself, a trifle jovial and a trifle indifferent; perhaps not too bad when you think of it, and considering he has a well-toned body too, I could well imagine girls may find him attractive, though not all the rage perhaps. Regardless of whether he had been with Elif on the jetty, they would certainly make a handsome couple.

"What was it like?" I asked politely, after the dolphin restored him to us. In fact, I sympathised a great deal with this animal. Intelligent as you are held to be, gregarious too, what must it be like to squander your life on something as meaningless as swimming in circles with tourists hanging from your fin? Sorry, I concluded, no dolphin ombudsman, not even in the EU, which otherwise does all sorts of things.

Carlos draped himself in a big Singapore Airlines towel, feeling cold it seemed, as he hadn't exerted himself at all in the water.

Positioning himself in the sun, he says:

"Got a message this morning that I have to go back to Australia soon."

This doesn't seem to surprise Madeleine at all, and perhaps

she already knew.

"It's to defend my thesis and for a graduation ceremony."

"Where is this?" I asked.

"Well, Hobart, not a well-known place. You don't have to tell me it's not on a level with MIT or Chicago," he said, shaking water firmly out of his ears.

I didn't know what MIT stood for, but wisely refrained from guessing.

"I'm not in a position to have any opinion on that except that it is sound to mistrust rankings."

"Uh-huh. Anyway, it has the edge on the behavioural perspective, rather than marginal productivity, input-output and such old-saws."

Abracadabra to me.

We found a restaurant in the centre with tables spread out on the pavement, ordered a range of small Turkish dishes and sat down to wait for the owner to come out with a tray to choose from. This is a small and simple eating place but the *mezeler* are homemade and almost never let you down. Indeed, they were delicious; never mind the tourists zigzagging around us, many Germans but fewer Russians these days. Behind us there was a juice stand, and we ordered *nar*, pomegranate.

"Birger, in your companies, when new leaders are taken on, what qualifications are you looking for in the first place? I mean, considering we have had a financial crisis, real estate bubbles, you name it, for quite some time now."

Not having an answer to his question, I said: "Turkey, for one, has weathered it fairly well."

"Is that right? Anyway, it's absolutely necessary to put an end to this *herd behaviour*. Business needs independent-minded people, not least banks do."

I nodded a little absent-mindedly. Not vertically, some other direction.

"This guy, Madoff," he continued, "heard of him? The one with the pyramid scheme. People continued to buy his securities because everyone else did. Amazing, like a flock of sheep, they walked into the trap."

"Brought to the pyramid fold," I suggested.

"Yea, yea! Sixty-five billion dollars down the drain. Absolutely laughable."

He pursed his mouth and produced a hissing sound.

"But, Birger, what d'you think of *sangfroid*?"

Sangfroid? His question came from a sky as blue as the one above us, my thoughts having strayed to what had happened after the fraudster's conviction: his belongings up for auction; studs and watches, even his shoes, as if his owning them had added value to them. After the flock of sheep, the pack of jackals.

"You mean staying calm in a situation…" I began, "or controlling your feelings in a situation of…"

"Exactly."

"Well…"

Carlos took over. "I find *sangfroid* extremely important, you know. You may see it as a dimension of an *independent mind*, right? Now, the question is, how to find an indicator of it? You know what I mean? If the whites of the eyes are yellow, that's of course a fairly clear sign you are not okay. How would you say we might find out if someone is prone to lose his head in a crisis?"

I took a draught of the red elixir. Then another. A man in a white jacket, with hairy eyebrows and fingers, had squeezed it for me, no sugar added, and now he was smiling at me behind his piles of *nar* and oranges. My drink was terribly sour, which I hadn't expected. Wholesome all right, but gives me the creeps. Carlos' project does too: similarly wholesome?

"Well, search me," I said.

Self-control and yellow eyes, I reflected. Last time these ideas were brought up, it was fever and blood tests. Presently, I came up with something to say:

"I have heard of personality tests? Psychologists do them, don't they?"

"No, no. What they do comes down to asking people to tell us their own opinion on how they will manage with their backs against the wall. Psychologists are of no use, captive to their own unimaginative conventions."

*

His talking points were inspiring, although not necessarily in the way he may have wished. Would three neophytes do a better job than an experienced psychologist? What on earth do they want? If something less conventional, there is always iris analysis and palm reading! Besides, there was something strange about it all. All the *sangfroid* bankers and others that the newspapers keep writing about with super-size bonuses and mega pots of pension gold, wreaking havoc nonetheless; shouldn't such be cut out in the first place?

This and more came to me only on our ride back from Kash, when it would have been provocative to bring it up, and also unwise on account of my neck. How I wish it were that of a snake bird, that I was free to govern ruthlessly (and my stomach that of a crocodile's).

With my lack of interest in enterprise – which may or may not have been brought home to Carlos by now – I am no source for him to scoop tips or contacts from. Even as an interlocutor, I am without merit, unless prepared to smother my views as soon as they are at variance with his, which is certainly trying for a person like me who is used to speaking his mind. Or was? In my earlier days, I would have taken it as an opportunity for behavioural therapy, but I have already drawn the line; you can't do CBT all your life!

"As for tonight," Madeleine said when we began to see the village and Liman in the distance, the minaret roof illuminated by the setting sun, "the fridge is empty. Eggs and a chocolate bar, that's all we've got. One or two carrots perhaps."

"Chocolate omelette," I blurted out, briskly and joyfully in spite of nausea brewing. "With carrot sticks."

After a while, Carlos said in a rather low pitch: "There's a Pizza Hut a few miles on."

"Yes, I know," Madeleine answered, "but you do like Turkish food, don't you?"

"It's okay, except that yoghurt ruined with water."

"So, let's go to the hotel, the best cook around here."

"The hotel. You mean the one with the mega-sized portico, turban or whatever, where you get your mail?"

"Yes, it's part of our lives here, so we never use its name."

"That dark-skinned waiter isn't exactly a success story," Carlos mumbled, as if talking to himself, but Madeleine could hear it, and even I as we were now slowly and almost noiselessly rolling down from the main road.

" Zia? He steps in sometimes, but his real job is gardening and maintenance work."

"I don't understand that man. He is always trying to strike up a conversation and I lose my grip on it after two words, just get pissed off with him. Pig Latin. Certainly not English!"

"No problem, Carlos. You can have a beer or some wine and leave the talking to me."

He was agitated, querulous, I guessed, more because we did not care to humour him than because of Zia. In any event, he wouldn't have met Zia that frequently. Or would he?

*

For me, as for Mark Twain, humour is a great thing.

Madeleine asked me how my endoscopy had gone –irritable bowel.

"Oh, wonderful! A tip-top clinic, you know, the doctor was driving his little camera like a rally car in there. Bumpy road, I can tell you, skilled at cornering he was. Everything perfect! I could follow it on a screen."

I paused for a moment.

"In fact, I asked for the DVD… So let's watch it tonight!" Madeleine exploded with laughter. Carlos wasn't on the same wavelength, but I can't change my personality just because he is in the house, can I?

8

One week later, Carlos cleared out, leaving a suitcase behind. He didn't say if or when he would return; "it all depends on my discussions with my colleagues."

The day before, we had gone together to the market in a neighbouring village because he wanted to buy homemade Turkish delight – a popular candy made of starch and sugar, often honey, rosewater and chopped nuts too –which was one of the few things in this country he had heaped praise on. His idea was for Madeleine and I to certify the quality of these flower-sugared cubes and take care of the haggling.

In a sparse pine wood with around fifty stands, Turkish delight was sold on more than ten, but whether it was homemade was difficult to tell. The female vendors' harem pants and headscarves were not to be banked on; nor that the candy boxes looked homemade, put together from simple strips of wood; repackaging is a simple thing.

It was as difficult for him to choose as it was for us to hammer out a deal. At length, we got away with six little wooden crates from as many stands; five for his upcoming seminar and one for his helpers. We have a feeling he has a sweet tooth.

Behind the stands there was a caravan from which tea was being served. You had to find your own seat, and a worn-down millstone was good enough for us. We sat down with our tulip-shaped glasses and a bowl of brown semolina cookies soaked in syrup (*shekerpare*) while the stack of Turkish delight was safely parked at Carlos' feet; no ants as far as the human eye could see.

We were all absorbed in our thoughts, and I felt the situation a little oppressive – our last outing and we had nothing to say.

"Tell us, why you chose an MBA?"

After my cogitation, I thought this opening had come out quite well. From the top drawer even. Later on, in hindsight, Carlos' decision would perhaps stand out as one of the most decisive in his life.

"Well, why not?"

I didn't expect this volley and needed a moment to think it over. "I take it there were hundreds of other programmes to choose from?"

He shrugged a shoulder, as if in agreement, and then moved to an upturned wooden box, for onions or potatoes or something, which, shaky as it was, to my mind did not seem much of an improvement on the millstone. Unless he did it out of concern for his candy stacks, which he put up on the place he had just vacated.

I tried a change of tack. "I guess one might easily come up with a score of good reasons for picking an MBA?"

"Really?"

Not exactly being prompted by him, I started to list them anyhow. "Economists make money, everyone knows that. And in case you like travelling, you would like to join a multinational corporation, and an MBA would give you an admission ticket to that. Right?"

I was picking up steam.

"Getting a prestigious, academic title, such as MBA, might be for some a dream from boyhood," I suggested, suppressing *far better than a Harley Davidson*. "Then again, if it's about making a difference in this world, a practically inclined economist may have better chances than most, I guess. As a researcher too.

"This world, according to many," I continued, "is economy-driven. Both Marx and liberal economists can shake hands on that. Hence, logic would favour an MBA? What do you think."

Carlos was young enough not to have any age-related wrinkles; nor were there any others to be seen. In fact, I found his face now had an unusually smoothed-out aspect.

It came to me... "For anyone like you, Carlos, thanks to your fascination with computers and IT, a business degree could well be a way of pursuing this interest further." I had determined that it was important for my point – whatever it had been – to surpass half a score at a minimum, but now, after fewer than ten reasons, I felt my engagement straggling.

It might be, also, I put forward, a bit more philosophically, that one wants to see a particular place, a beautiful landscape or wide beaches, whatever –where they happen to have an MBA programme too?

At this moment, there was a change in Carlos' face, or so I fancied; he was following me a bit more keenly, so I decided to have another turn at it: "Well, it might be that you had been working on a cattle farm or as a bartender or something in a place like, say, Christchurch, and had got some money in hand and you met someone, who in fact had passed that same programme in Hobart... Or else this person was on his way there – or her way, as the case may be – and you told yourself: why not?"

Carlos gave a grin; if weak, a grin it was.

"I give you credit for your last guess. In fact, I was in Auckland for an interview with Qantas – the airline, you know, with a kangaroo on the tail fin. Never mind, I got a cheap ticket to Tasmania and in transit in Sydney – I met someone who gave me some information about this Hobart programme."

"A girl perhaps?"

He took a sip and that was that.

My powers of judgement, I should say, are generally sound, but latecomers; my feelings are twice as quick. No doubt, this was an ill-considered question.

We had breakfast and walked to the spot at the head of our little settlement where the rubbish bins are kept and taxis wait for their customers. The drivers won't venture into the narrow, winding drive between the houses, as the turnaround at the far end is frequently full of innovatively parked cars. Likewise, Comet's big dumper takes up space from time to time, somehow on his sister's account – Fatosh, I mean, who lives here, whereas he doesn't.

The tombola-like containers are, in Madeleine's and my view, not Carlos', quite decorative, and inevitably bring to mind the luminous green bugs that thrive in these parts. Tolerably odour-free, too, when the lids are well closed.

Carlos said:

"Really, I fail to understand why you settled here."

I was startled. It came out of thin air, never having heard him say anything like this before. Was this something he had been puzzling over, not knowing the answer or finding a clue? Was it really? Maybe he was just unfavourably impressed by something else, like yesterday's conversation in the market? Or was it due to the bins, or at least triggered by them, from which a foul smell was actually leaking out?

No offence could be seen on Madeleine's face, though she was a little goggle-eyed:

"You find it as bad as that?" Whereas I, touched on the raw, would have preferred something like: *I'll make a note of that: how'd you score it out of ten?* She added:

"There had to be a drastic shift, you know. We had to make a move."

"Okay, but why this backwoods place? No communications,

no services. No social life, I guess. Nothing. Except the sea."

Madeleine's voice still calm: "Against these incommodities, do you think fresh air and calm weigh as nothing?" Well, the quality of the air may not carry much weight right now, I reflected.

"Yea, fresh air all right, but damp even in winter."

"Whether dampness is an upside or a downside depends on your health," I interposed, having Madeleine's skin in mind, of course.

"A two-and-a-half-hour drive to an airport!" he insisted.

I felt called upon to say something also on this count: "Not so bad. After all, it would take you just as long if you lived in Ankara." He scanned my face for a moment, perhaps challenging my comparison, his eyes narrowing a little behind his glasses. Our discussion died a death.

Caught by an impulse of jocularity, I decided to breathe new life into it: "You must give us credit for such a spacious bathroom as we have here. In no other…"

Now he appeared rather to open his eyes wide. Perhaps just my imagination again, but I was fearful lest I was making a bad mistake. So instead of completing my sentence, with *In no other will you find nearly as many loo rolls stacked up*, I shifted feet as quickly as a professional windsurfer: "Yes, truly, in no other place can you buy such delicious Turkish delight."

*

Across the bushland down to the beach, our eyes followed the rolling of the taxi's dust cloud. Even if Carlos was waving back at us, we wouldn't see it.

"How wonderful that he is doing so well," said Madeleine.

"Indeed, and that he didn't get his degree out of gold fever."

While returning to the house, I added: "Sometimes he

exudes a good deal of self-confidence." She nodded and I sent up a trial balloon.

"Could do with a little less, perhaps?"

"Better than diffidence, I should say."

I opted for one more, less conspicuous.

"Carlos said he was writing a thesis together with two others. A business idea, he said."

"What of it?"

"Playing fast and loose with borrowed money, which it has to be, is always risky."

"Okay, Birger. You weren't like that at all, and where did that get you?" she said with a big smile.

Madeleine has solid rabbit front teeth, still white, and Carlos has strong teeth too. Just me who has a set of teeth of less-than-dazzling whiteness.

"I don't follow."

"You used to say that your inventions would have lied fallow unless Jens and I, rather bluntly, had taught you there was ploughing too."

The last words came out almost separately.

"Yes, yes, I'm no ploughman, never was perhaps. But there is also sowing; and what Carlos and his pals have to put in the furrows, that's what we don't know."

Other things were on Madeleine's mind right now.

In an hour, she would meet her Facebook friends, the *Moth and Bird Group,* who were going to a site near Demresi to see the *six-spot burnet*. "Very, very beautiful," she had declared, and almost rhythmically declaimed: "two red wings, two green wings with dark red spots, certainly not enough to see them on a computer screen."

"It's just that I can't get it out of my head that I could somehow or other be drawn into this," I said. "And besides, it's a pity to get into risky loans at such a young age."

"Yes, you have said that."

Carlos' future was of course a sensitive matter for her. For me too, as I had put a fly in her ointment.

I took a morning mountain walk. The sun was on its way up behind the cliff in the bay. Towing some sort of cleaning implement, a tractor was driving about on the beach with a troop of expectant stray dogs in its wake. I drank in the view of the sea from my favourite plateau, while at the same time a certain ease invaded me. It was less from the glittering expanse than from the pureness of the air. And yet not – it was Carlos.

PART II

9

The sun pushed up behind the big cliff in the middle of the bay, lending it an aura that grew by the minute. It was set to be a nice day, not least for those who would be touring the nearby Greek isles on the old but well-kept two masted *gülel* moored some fifty metres out from the jetty. Though residing in this hamlet for two years now, we have never made this trip, and the brisk-eyed captain, who happens to live just two houses down from us, has finally stopped pestering us about it.

While Madeleine is swimming, I usually do exercises on the beach for half an hour or so, which is what she normally needs for her skin as well as her mental composure. Not today. No exercises, since I am experimenting with new creams and so have to protect my *trial areas* on legs and arms, not least in view of the risk that stray dogs may take my high kicking and waving arms for invitations to play.

These have not been lazy days. I was in need of a greenhouse and had an architect from Izmir take a look at the back of our house, which has a southern aspect, and make a sketch.

My 'fortune', as I have already hinted, is founded on the sale of some pharmaceutical discoveries to do with unknown agave plants. I sold these and bought a stake in a company, well, more than one as it turned out later. I'm still interested in these plants today, fortunately. You have to take care of your interests in later years, or pretty quickly you may end up going without.

However, I had overestimated the number of sunshine hours, simply because I hadn't taken into consideration the mountains all around. There was a further problem. This architect, trim linen shirt, beautifully patterned Turkish waistcoat, eau de cologne, couldn't find the property boundaries. No need for such niceties, say people round here, on the grounds that the unkempt land beyond our gardens has no owner, and their own rather gutsy expansions of their plots underscore this, one neighbour even having a paddock laid out. My architect, however, would not draw anything that stretched beyond the property line.

He was a cultivated man who stayed for coffee and a cigar, his own: "Human endeavour doesn't acknowledge *horror vacui*: there is no such thing as ownerless soil. Property lines may often be invisible but they are never unimportant. I've seen half-metre encroachments wreak havoc among men."

After a few weeks' deadlock, Zia came over and told me a cousin of his, a vegetable grower on a large scale, would be happy to give me a hand.

Volkan was short and plump with a black beard sprouting in all directions, closely resembling an Islamic fundamentalist disguised in a baggy, dark costume. Later, I disclosed my and Madeleine's anxieties to Zia. He dissolved into laughter: "No, my cousin is completely irreligious – fundamentally irreligious, ha ha – but irritated by shaving."

The contract was drawn up by Abdullah, the bank manager in the village. While Volkan and I read through the document, he sat soft-eyed and unmovable behind his painted metal desk. No one can sit as still as Abdullah.

I got to know him when we settled down here and our savings came under the care of his office, next to the Atatürk monument, in the cobblestoned village square. For several years, there were two photo frames in front of him, his dead wife and his daughter, but on this occasion his wife had moved to the wall near the window facing the small banking hall, while another woman, unknown to me, had replaced her in the desk frame. Our relationship had changed over time, to friendship now, and I very much hoped he had met someone who cared for him.

It so happened that when the idea came to me to support the Madan Mogra Orphanage, Abdullah became my sounding board as well as my travelling companion to India – Madeleine, Jens and Euphemia, Jen's wife, came along too, quite a delegation as it were – and ever since, Abdullah has been in charge of the *Ivar Foundation*, named after our small textile mouse, through which money is siphoned to the orphanage. This is more or less the only economic enterprise I have been fully engaged in. When, on our first visit there, I fished Ivar out of my shirt pocket among all the children and officials for him to be inspected and admired, a storm of cheering burst out, never to be forgotten; certainly, that was where he had come into existence. At that moment, it had struck me that my depression was definitely under control.

It had been a taxing day. We had been travelling for hours in an overheated train, prior to walking along a dusty street to the orphanage under the glowing midday sun. Ivar was the only one not dripping with sweat. He looked really dapper in his ruby-red dress with yellow tucker.

Once a year, I go to Madan Mogra for the Annual Meeting and it will soon be time for it again. I have tried to nudge Abdullah to accompany me, the travelling is much more pleasant with him by my side; but as he is a gentle person, I refrain from saying so outright. He knows my ways and has promised to give it some thought; I guess he finds it wasteful for us both to go.

One more thing on my agenda: if I am really serious about this greenhouse, I should systematically scrutinise old replies from laboratories and establish new contacts with them. This would also mean roaming more intensely through my old, secret habitats. Except that some of them are in war zones, meaning that Madeleine would put her foot down immediately; she wouldn't dream of coming with me and would never allow me to go alone, which I wouldn't like to anyway. It is important to protect one's interests; but at such an inflated price?

10

Carlos was back.

I had just picked up the mail at the hotel and chatted a little with Zia – not about the Kurdish question this time or Turkey's, slim, chances of joining the EU, but about an overcrowded refugee boat sighted off the lighthouse. From a distance, I recognised Carlos from his gait, which imitates a sort of wave motion – a jump forward and up and down at the same time, like an ostrich, which comes of putting down the toes before the heels.

He had his red rucksack over one shoulder, was wearing a peaked cap and mirror sunglasses, and carrying two gadgets, one in each hand, alternately busying himself with each, speaking into both. *Multi-tasking*, is that what they call it now? While I waited for him at the driveway to our clump of houses, it dawned on me that one of them was something he was eating from: could be an ice cream from the nearest grocery. Truth be told, my vision had improved following cataract surgery, but there was still a need for a tidy-up behind the plastic lens (called a capsulotomy, I have been told), and I hadn't got round to going to Ankara yet; that is, I hadn't listed the books I would buy as I was wont to do whenever I went there.

"Have you got the measles?" he said, sucking on his Magnum Classic. This was the first banter he had tried on me as a grown-up, a bit forced perhaps, but banter nonetheless. I couldn't help laughing, although for some reason it came out harder than it should.

I had plasters all over my arms and was wearing a t-shirt that found room for quite a few.

"Well, if not measles, then some other blister, but don't worry, it's not infectious."

That he had returned just to pick up his luggage was unlikely. His suitcase (heavy with books and electronic devices?) was still standing in the corner on the second floor where he had left it, and we had been ready to send it as soon as we got his accommodation address. Maybe it was for the sake of Elif. Anyway, without even a decent pub or a café, our small borough couldn't be a base for anything that an ambitious young man would set his mind to, unless he needed us for some reason.

His seminar had gone like clockwork, 'fabulous', and now there was some further thinking to do. A little breathing time so to speak, for things to 'crystallise a bit'.

I took on the part of a well-mannered and interested listener, asking feel-good questions. Sounds like you got a heap of good ideas, right? Is it difficult to coordinate work on a thesis with the work of others? Nice people? I tried to put in a quip: personal chemistry is always tricky. We can't make gold; we are not all alchemists. Was there a party afterwards? With the teachers, and tutors?

His responses slowed after a while, perhaps finding fault with my asking. I took care to avoid questions that might bring forth answers likely to *dis-poise* me, if there is such a word; I wasn't all that keen to hear details about their 'great bandying of ideas'.

*

It appeared his seminar gave him a shot in the arm.

"You know, there were high-profile people visiting us."

"Oh, you don't say?"

"I guess you have heard of Dr Vorster, the branding guru? With Einstein hair?"

"I don't think so, really."

"A funny little man, he is, but very sharp. He gave one of his famous lectures on personal branding. In Sydney."

"Aha."

"There was this Swedish minister, Dr Vorster told us, a social democrat, who was dumped by the government. Moana Salin was her name. And so she set out to start a company."

"Rings a bell," I got out; only a weak one, though.

"Remember her business idea? 'My business idea,' she said, 'is Moana Salin!'"

He looked at me half triumphantly, without my understanding why.

I couldn't share his enthusiasm. Incidentally, it wasn't Moana. It was Mona. The mispronunciation – perhaps this Vorster's work – had a Polynesian ring to it. Students are generally not former Cabinet Ministers, of course, I remarked, so I guess somehow you will have to make a name for yourself first, cashing in on it at a later date. Long haul.

No, no, no!

He shook his head more vigorously than an older person would ever venture to do; in fact, to a degree that made me shudder. Shrink, too, to be honest.

"That's not fair to young talents," he said forcefully. "The other way around it has to be: they will have to start with the brand, you see! One would want a level playing field, right?"

I kept my counsel. I fancied he looked at me the way you look at a Henry Moore: what could the sculptor have conceivably meant by it?

Carlos' ways began to conflict with mine in our 'little' house; mostly with his telephone. He dominated the living room like a regiment posted on a hill. His telephone postures were no less of a nuisance.

Leaning back on the larger sofa, mobile in his left hand, the other hand more often than not wandering down the back of his neck hunting for pimples, or else fingering some IT what-not on the table. Sometimes his feet on the table, a very beautiful piece of furniture that we treasure a lot.

Why he was telephoning in the house was beyond me, as he would get much better reception outside. It couldn't be because of the weather, which was as nice as nice can be. Not yet too hot, and ideal for sitting out of doors; the pine fragrance had begun to yield to mimosa and there were notes of citrus in the air. It wasn't early spring any longer.

Sometimes he left the house, of course, more or less like before but far less frequently and not for long; not carrying much, either.

I asked Madeleine what Carlos was planning to do next. Did she know? She was probably right that, lately, I had been talking to him more often than she, who had had a stint in Side, which is too far for commuting.

"Anyway, Carlos would rather tell you than me," I said and a joke sprang into my head. "Usually, you know... he tells me as good as nothing unless I ask. If I do, he tells me twice as much. Two times zero so to speak." I giggled a little.

"Don't be finicky now. He's not so good at explaining things, that's all. And no wonder, that's what it's like when you are so absorbed in your own thinking. You must have experienced it too."

That may be so, yes...

I played with the thought of confessing that there had actually been a limit to my questions to him, to how much I wanted to hear from him, but put it out of my mind, unwilling to be pushed for an explanation. Not to be done in a hurry.

11

Had Carlos ever told me the name of his university? I thought not, and as the mists should be dispelled I chanced to just google his name.

Much to my surprise, there were several hits. All of them brought me to one and the same homepage, however: groups of merry teachers and students spread out on a lawn – as if laughing away the labour of the learning day – with a stately brick façade looming in the background. Across the picture, in calligraphic style, ran *South Australia Business Academy*. From the *About Us* link, I learned that this was a *relatively new, dynamic e-university with a special focus on challenging…*

I wouldn't read it all. Although alone in the house, I wanted it over and done with as quickly as possible. So I surfed on: *General Description, Programmes, Services, Student Portal, Contact…* and then I was brought back to the start page. On this round trip, there had been no mention of a street address, only mailing addresses. Curious, I thought, rather like a wheel with a tyre and spokes but no hub.

And what became of Carlos? And his two fellow students? I would certainly pursue the search – without fear or favour, I enticed myself – and however it came about, he turned up, sort of out of the blue, under the heading *MBA, Practical Application*, together with other names, all of them with personal presentations.

Carlos, I learned, was 'formerly in the air transport industry, graduating this summer from *South Australia Business Academy*. Master's thesis part of the major project: Leadership in a World of Flux'.

Armed with this, it was easy enough to identify his two partners: Tarek Sayedi had conducted 'studies at the faculty of philosophy at Cairo University', held an 'honorary degree from the University of Karachi' and was also a 'successful chess tournament player'. Ben Smith had a background as a 'SANDF army officer' (what's that?) and made 'regular appearances on television' in the Southern Africa region.

I had to reread it. To the best of my knowledge, Carlos' experience of the 'air transport industry' boiled down to occasional work behind airline counters. And what would an honorary degree from Karachi stand for?

Well, graduates today are apt to think highly of themselves, that they are entering a higher rank of life. Maybe in the process they find it natural to upgrade their backgrounds too.

I let it go. A couple of clicks brought me to *Major Projects,* their graduate work. Whereas all the text so far had been black on a white background, this was now green on a black background; *green's the colour of the surgeons* ran through my head (can't help it, occupational hazard).

But I couldn't give this surgeon text more than a brief glance because there were sounds coming from the hall downstairs. Immediately, I pressed ctrl+alt+delete. But mine is an aged computer and even for this mayday command, it needs to think the matter over.

It was unlikely to be Madeleine, since she would have saluted me loudly on entering the house. Whoever it was, this person seemed hesitant. I rose abruptly from my chair, which responded with a rasping creak and spared me the trouble of coming up with a cough or something.

The lightest of steps were heard downstairs.

A little muzzle appeared at the bend of the staircase, then a bit more. I recognized the stray puppy I had seen at the fringes of the canine packs at the seashore. She had followed me into our street once and looked rather civilised, even if a little dusty. On perceiving her behind me, Fatosh, Madeleine's neighbour-friend, who usually claims expertise only in gardening, had said: "A hefty dose of Border Terrier in that one, blech!"

I took offence for some reason or other, and tried the facetious way: "And who of us isn't a bit borderline, may I ask?" but she wasn't at all receptive.

Though this little creature had certainly not been invited, indeed came at a critical juncture, I could by no means be cross with her. She continued to climb and I let her come up to the landing, where she sat down and yawned widely a couple of times, a chasm of imposing teeth for her size, all the while fixing her eyes on me, while turning her head on one side.

I took her up in my arms and prattled to her on the way out. She has long black lashes above small eyes and wiry hair, but her ears are smooth and shiny, silken. All the way to the dustbins I took her, tore off a tick from her nose, and put her down.

Without too much trouble, I returned to the web pages, and there I was now with Carlos *et consortes* in glaring green before me and – not what I was used to at this time of the year – behind closed doors; the front door shut, but not locked of course.

Leadership in a World of Flux (LEADWOF)

As the volatility of business environments are ratcheting up in permanent globalisation processes, *leadership recruitment* up to now has proved increasingly defective at focusing on the refinement of human capital through education and training, while neglecting the crucial side of *raw-material screening* and so needs to be substituted for a new, holistic paradigm.

In **Leadwof**, Carlos Edman, Tarek Sayedi and Ben Smith take up the gauntlet to elaborate novel *and* cost-effective strategies for the optimization of high level, executive HR recruitment.
Click *here for the three sub-projects*. NB! Full text of these studies is restricted in view of potential commercial confidentiality.

A language check would not have gone amiss; I established that, but otherwise could make neither head nor tail of it; nor was I in the mood to give decoding a try, so I opted for the *Click here* suggestion.

The first study had the rather colourless title *Human Resources – Human Challenges: An Overview,* whereas the second was entitled *In Quest of Winning Horses.* Obviously, bringing to bear the other two, the third part contained *innovative business proposals.* These *dynamic* proposals stated that *three different strategies for raising capital* were to be followed, *payback period-wise on very favourable terms.*

Full of confused impulses, I had started to swivel back and forth in my desk chair. The squeaking was grating on my nerves, and I couldn't overcome my impatience. I should take a rest.

I had sat down at the PC before noon, and the sun had gone around the edge of the window, so it was past two-thirty now. This was unknown to the computer, its own clock having been all at sea for many years. Not only the desk chair was on the brink of the grave.

If nothing else, this Leadwof, I thought, is a significant push for the number three. There are three students, three sub-projects and three strategies; business suggestions too, presumably. Astrologers would set great store by this.

It was *In Quest of Winning Horses* that drew my attention the most. Not that I knew what a 'winning horse' was, but this much seemed clear: those who could find them were, themselves, little more than sucking colts.

The brief text squared strikingly well with what Carlos had been canvassing for so enthusiastically; thermometers, sedimentation tests and all that… If he wasn't the sole author, at least he was a prominent co-author, I thought, without much satisfaction.

I began to find this *Academy* homepage wrapped if not in mystery, then at least in inexactitudes, or perhaps something even less palatable.

No no! I wouldn't be the one to sow seeds of doubt. On the contrary, I would put the best construction on it. As far as inexactness went, the reason might be, indeed probably is, to get visitors to the homepage, make contact, get hold of them in a way they wouldn't otherwise.

I switched off, for good this time. Not my business: to each his own worry.

*

My reaction was facile – the coin landing on the side of self-comforting nonchalance, but it was less than a day before the flip side of weakness came up.

That this trio was set on starting something up, I could confidently assume, along the lines of the acronym which had already slipped my mind, *Wolf…* something.

Three funding strategies there were. And what's the meaning of it? That financing would be brotherly shared, one-third falling to Carlos' lot? Pure coincidence, or more than coincidence?

I didn't suppose Carlos had much money to put on the table; he would certainly have to borrow the lion's share, or even all of it.

Loans on *very favourable terms*, what to believe about that? That the money will be quickly reimbursed? Could be, and, if so, because they reckon on hefty profits? Small beer, they may think, these guys, as they are (or think themselves) both 'innovative' and 'dynamic'.

And which creditors does Carlos have in mind?

People like me would have to take it on trust, though trust, unfortunately, is not my forte, my knowledge of economics equally infirm.

The more I turned all this over in the brain-tumbler, the more convinced I was that I should seek counsel. Abdullah could debunk it for me. But on second thoughts, no; a rather sensitive person, he wouldn't appreciate being consulted on a matter like this.

In his local savings bank, he had been leading a quiet life, mostly routine, when I offered him a chance to grapple with something more challenging. He would take a chunk of my deposits to try his fortune, and mine, on the stock market. This he did masterfully, but full of anxiety and wanting to quit. So it would have to be Jens.

If your son, Jens – well, he only has a daughter – had just got an e-MBA, how much money would you be willing to cough up for the plan he has cooked up with his pals? As it is a graduate thesis project, they should have put their best foot forward. To me, it is *hallux valgus*.

I imagined him pacing up and down in his CEO room in Geneva asking for more details. Earphone, mild voice. When I first met him, at a London conference, neither of us was at our best. It turned out he had had depression, like me, but his recovery was further advanced. Since London, a growing bald patch has appeared on the crown of his head – which may explain why he has grown a beard, so richly and tightly woven that you don't really see where his mouth is until it opens and you get this funny Eureka feeling.

"Jens, one more thing. What's this about quick reimbursement? Repayment must depend on incomes flowing in, mustn't it? Counting chickens before they are hatched?"

12

Every time Carlos' mobile rang, it punished my ears – a signal like from a demolition derby. He went out onto the terrace, on and off, but *de facto* had put down stakes in the living room. In there, he used a much stronger voice than outdoors, whereas the reverse seems more natural, at least it is for all the Turks I know, bar that grocer Madeleine and I have nicknamed Shortchanger, who squeals his head off whether inside his shop or outside.

I tried to disconnect him, so to speak, but the stairs to the second floor were a willing herald for his messages. From my office, I overheard large chunks of his conversations, even when I set my teeth against it, in particular when he was talking with his two pals – the one from Egypt, Tarek, wasn't it, although Carlos called him Teddy, and the other, Ben.

"How are things going?"
Pause.
"How many have you got so far?"
Pause.
"Great. Of these, how many commitments?"
Pause.
"So the early bird rate wouldn't…?"
Short pause.
"Wow!"

Carlos, always leaning back on the sofa, had his feet by turns on the floor and on the coffee table, which I could see every time I sneaked a look at him. Naturally, I worried for Ivar, who always stands leaning against a Wedgwood bowl in the middle of the table, and for that matter, for the bowl as well, if I'm honest. It was a 50th birthday gift to Madeleine, celestial dragons on it, its green metallic glaze matching Ivar's red and yellow. True, I don't have much day-to-day contact with Ivar these days, but for me he is still what the Lincoln statue is for a true American: the 'Great Emancipator'. He was a support for me during my recovery and embodies the orphanage project in India.

"If, for curiosity's sake, you could just mail me a list?"

Pause.

"Don't bother. Just company names."

Long pause.

"Sort of a kick seeing ducklings lined up in a row."

I felt it trying to listen to these conversations. Must have struck a raw nerve, of which I have several, and my solution was to decamp on such occasions; a mountain walk or a bicycle ride to somewhere for a cappuccino, or something that at least bears resemblance to one; mostly counterfeits around here.

There were even more distracting variants.

"Given any more thought to *Sangfroid* and *Stability*?"

Pause.

"Oh yes, as many indicators as possible. Distribution of them not an issue at this stage, right?"

Long pause.

"So Teddy's father is… thrilled to bits, did you say?"

Pause.

"Yea, couldn't agree more. And a fine job he did about the lawyers and everything."

Long pause.

"Just a few more thoughts about the order of…"

Pause.

"That, exactly. By the way, I find *fire evacuation* really good, the very best even in that category, although not as a starter of course. And, sure thing, figurants. Feinter wanted! Ha, ha, ha…"

It was after a couple of days of the more unbalancing kind that I went to the village market, the *Pazar*, which I seldom do. On hearing the ringing of the little yellow Toyota bus, market shuttle today, otherwise school bus, outside the hotel, I darted off to intercept it. A sudden urge to escape alone could not explain this impulse. There was also the idea in the back of my head of buying underwear and peeled pistachios for a nutty cake. At least I like to remember it that way. North Cypriot brandy for the cake was already waiting in the scullery, and we always keep a reassuring stock of antacids.

It's the kind of weekday market you find in thousands of places in Turkey, located on some unused piece of land with wooden stakes pounded into the ground to sustain sunshades, this one situated just outside the village, by a bend in a stream (which ultimately falls out into the bay in Liman, where we live), with the myrtle-enclosed village cemetery close by, with which it shares both water and toilets. I make my way down the wide aisle with textile handicrafts. No real crowds yet; knots of tourists examine the embroidered cloth and bed covers, beautiful and pricey, leaving *salwar trousers*, headscarves and what-not to their fate.

Furthest down, at the short side, I find an electronics stall, which is both a long counter resting on trestles and an altered VW campervan, with a long fold-down desk on the outside, part of the wall, for the display of mobile phones, the inside crammed with assorted cartons.

"I'm looking for something that can obstruct a telephone," I tell the two men who are sitting smoking on camping stools at the back of the vehicle, "something which stops it working."

They just looked at me like they didn't catch on.

"Which stops it," I try again, "like when you don't want the children to use the phone."

They look Turkish all right, traditional mustachoes, and speak to each other in something sounding like Turkish, but which isn't, could be Azerbaijani or some other Turkic language. Brothers, I guess, or cousins.

"*Jammer*," one of them says. "*Sinyal boğucu!*"

"Yes, have you got one?"

"It's illegal," he says, and gives the other a glance.

I cast my eyes around. There is a box marked 'PRO booster' on the long desk.

"If you have that thing, a booster, you must have a jammer too? For the sake of balance, sort of," I add, waving an index finger, crooked for extra emphasis, looking impish.

They twigged it and smiled a little.

I went up the next corridor, which was lined with sweet-smelling stalls of Turkish candy and pastries, a kaleidoscope of colours: dried fruits, *baklava*, Turkish delight, nuts – a crate filled to the brim with naked pistachios is a delight to the eye – wild herbs and fresh fruit. Less easy to get through here, Turks and tourists everywhere.

I buy a few hands of Mersin bananas, small fingers but far more tasty than their South American broiler cousins, and *fındık*, or pistachio, for the cake, and then saunter on, through the corridors, while applying my standard loafing trick – not listening to vendor calls, not understanding Turkish, not touching wares – until I ended up at the electronics stall again.

I said: "So you don't have it?"

"This is the kind of thing that those on high don't want you to have, no freedom in this country, Abi, big brother," says one of them, still sitting smoking, grinning like a guileful half-breed from some western of my youth.

"Look, if I can buy one, I certainly wouldn't tip anyone off. I give you my word. I kiss my dead baby…"

They called me big brother on account of my Turkish, I guessed, and now I had put confidence in the oath I had heard Fatosh's brother shouting when accused once of denting his sister's Hyundai (shabby as it was).

Anyway, it would be expensive.

"No problem," I said, fingers splayed, indicating I don't know what.

"Only cash," he said.

My nodding received and accepted, he got into the van and rummaged about. He handed me a box not much bigger than a pack of cigarettes, longer ones. Funny, my first cigarette was from this country – *39 Turk*, thin and very firmly rolled, so very difficult to keep lit.

I turned the box in my hands.

"It's Chinese?"

"Yes."

"Well, if they can build an aircraft carrier, they can make a little gadget like this."

They failed to see the humour in it; perhaps there was none.

*

I put the banana hands and pistachio bag on the kitchen counter, and the olive-picker on my workroom desk. The jammer I put at the very back of the desk drawer behind my passport and foreign money, together with Ivar's winter costume and sleeping bag.

I forgot to ask the *mustachiozillas* whether a telephone-user could detect a jammer in operation. I suppose I had better introduce it bit by bit, hit-and-run, so to speak.

13

Coming back from a visit to my greenhouses – yes, Volkan let me have a second, smaller one, too, free of charge, as if I was doing him a favour – Madeleine had some information for me.

"Carlos has moved."

"Done what?"

"Yes, moved to the village. Because it will make things easier."

"Hmm," I said, for want of something better. Not that I minded.

"Wouldn't like to be a bother, perhaps."

Bother? I shook my head rather more vigorously than intended, like when shaking off persistent carpet sellers outside the Blue Mosque.

Madeleine's face told me I had put my foot in it, so I had better explain: "look, sometimes I felt tired… more than that, of his telephoning." She had been working away from home for days and days on end now, and wouldn't know. But I had to make a stronger impression:

"It sometimes got on my nerves to the degree that I wanted a jammer."

"What's that?"

"A gadget that can block mobile phones."

"If you have been that irritated, you were really good at hiding it."

High praise indeed, though I couldn't resist asking: "Why? Easy to read my feelings, is that what you mean to say?"

"When you are upset, and I mean upset, your cheeks turn red – red and white, like fried bacon." Bacon? I felt piqued. People don't look like that; I tried to take the sting out of it. Not convinced I did by adding: "In fact, I bought one."

She gave me a glance of outright disbelief: "bullshit!"

Seldom if ever would she use this vocabulary; she would at most say 'crap', which is a word she inherited from her father, together with leanings towards pacifism, naturism and atheism. He was also a vegetarian, and possibly a communist, but those were never handed down to her.

Perhaps *bullshit* came from her recent work with people from… well, Australia or somewhere.

I told her about the market, the suspicion of the sellers and all. Her blue eyes were steadied on my face all the time and she said:

"It's illegal, you say, yet you could easily buy it! What a country this is!"

I was glad Turkey came in for its share. Hopefully, she would lose the thread.

"In Stockholm," I replied, "you don't have to walk more than one hundred yards from Central Station to buy a gun illegally."

She sighed, not for the first time during this conversation, and not necessarily from despondency or anger; physiotherapists know that sighing is like a reset button for your breathing and relaxation. "What a thing to do! How could you without even talking to Carlos first!"

"I never used it!"

"You meant to!"

"I didn't plan anything. And whatever I would have liked to do, my conscience would have probably put a stopper on it."

"Whatever, you should have talked to him."

We held our peace for a few moments. I couldn't keep my fingers away from a cutaneous horn, a sign of ageing, I suppose, on my left ear, as if to clear my mind. In fact, in these situations, a compulsion to kill it off – middle finger, fine weapon, its nail growing the fastest – easily takes over, which, vexingly enough, makes it harder for my thoughts to assert themselves.

"Maybe he wanted to get closer to Elif," Madeleine suggests.

I turned this conjecture over in my mind. I wouldn't be surprised if it came down to Carlos being *pushed* as much as pulled.

"No more than two kilometres closer," I said.

"Three miles," she replied.

"Well, I have a hunch these guys have something in preparation. Right here in Turkey."

"You don't say! How do you know?" she asked, tilting her head towards me a little. Her vision, if it comes to that, is excellent, another inheritance from her father, who as an old man could tell warblers from each other at a distance of 25 metres, in contrast to her mother, who was plagued by glaucoma.

"Well, how would I not?" I said with a somewhat laboured touch of regret. I feared she would reply: *You come down on him too often, don't you?* But she didn't.

If it so happens that when we have a big argument, flying at each other, and can't get out of it, there are two remedies; we go to bed, or we go for a strong latte somewhere, like to the nearest neighbouring village where since last year they can boast a good old-fashioned espresso machine, the pressure-cooker type. The mere cycle ride would make for a friendlier climate. Usually, riding behind Madeleine, I take delight in her movements on her ladder saddle with springs underneath. A little bit too high for her. She has nice legs for her age, particularly when tanned; never mind a few thin varicose veins, which after all are perceptible only to someone who already knows her intimately.

This time, we might not have been surly enough, or the matter wasn't so sensitive after all; or I may still have cherished the hope of her coming round to my way of thinking.

"I overheard his phone calls, you know. Well, that's not the word, actually; you don't overhear fanfares, you can't avoid listening to them; they are forced on you," I said with a smile that she would hopefully condone.

"Don't exaggerate… Besides, you have become rather sensitive to noise. You said so yourself, if you remember."

"Yes, yes. But you yourself must have heard… You didn't stay at Osman Excelsior all day, every day. Anyway, all of it was very much to my…"

"Your what?"

"It stirred feelings."

"Really?"

"Yes. In me."

I told her I had heard Carlos and his Duckburg pals – didn't use that word, just tempted to – discussing what business executives are like: executives suffer from herd behaviour, copying others because they distrust their own judgement – like buying or selling stocks or bonds just because others do. She gave me a furtive glance so I tried a trope closer to her passions: like a bird. Left alone, it knows exactly how to choose a safe nesting place, but seeing others choosing a poor one, it follows their example regardless. And then this trio say they are going to determine people's *capacity for independent behaviour.*

"What's the matter with that?" she said, spreading out her hands, the better to make clear her unreserved surprise.

When the eczema was at its worst, Madeleine's hands were always red and scaly, itchy too, of course, whereas now they could be used in an ad campaign for bridal rings; only they might be seen as a little on the broad side.

I didn't answer, as I had got worse up my sleeve.

"And they talk about gathering business people, for *Executive Coaching*, whatever that is, and staging *fire drills*!"

"I see no harm in that. Emergency training is customary! Earthquake, fire – I have done it several times at hotels and shouldn't be surprised if it is even prescribed."

"All right, but theirs is not a drill. It's reality, although all fake!"

Carlos' telephoning had been on my mind for weeks, but I had resolved not to precipitate any discussion about it with Madeleine and here I was up to my neck in it.

To pre-empt her glossing over this, too, I had to say more. Of course, an evacuation drill is in a way always fake, but this is not for training; it's to see people's reactions – whether they all scramble for the door, jamming exits or something, panicking, or keep their cool and even try to organise things, to take the lead, how would I know? Now, the idea is to weed out those who don't meet their criteria.

Plain as the nose on your face, she wasn't with me. I had no weight to throw around, no expertise, only an ugly feeling to share with her.

It wasn't as if I could hear a wailing warning siren, but it was more than a whimper, and if someone with just a smattering of economics had told me that their plans were but overbearing flummery cum hubris, I would have readily believed them and brought it to bear on Madeleine. Unfortunately, there was no one around, and although I had played with the idea of consulting with Jens, I had not made up my mind to do so.

"Birger," she said at last, "they are young." Nothing more.

This was a golden opportunity to put an end to our discussion, but I missed it.

"They want to blow their own horns, and what is there to toot about?"

I felt it wasn't the first time I had said this, so I filled the gap:

"They each have an MBA, so they fancy themselves an MBI too – *Master of Brilliant Intelligence*. Hey presto! The usual period of probation following graduation is superfluous."

"They have dreams, Birger. They can't be excoriated just for having dreams!"

"As long as they don't mistake them for reality. For one thing, suckling camel colts should—"

"Ah, all your *camelisms* and *frogisms* and *horseisms*, even real Turks don't talk like that!"

I was as flustered as she was, and thus entitled to raise my voice equally as much.

"Real Turks? Don't blame me if they squander their wonderful linguistic heritage. At least I won't! What's wrong with being naturalised anyway?"

A redness had come to her cheeks, as it had to mine too, I felt, and there was blood smeared on my middle fingertip, from my ear. I bent it towards the palm, locking the thumb over it.

"Okay, he is young," I said, my transmogrified hand lying turned up on my lap, "but youth cannot be an argument. Can it? I'm sure I don't excuse my own sillinesses as a youth, much less those when supposedly a mature man. Yet, I don't lay claim to maturity even now." Again I was repeating myself. She was quite right to be bored stiff.

*

It occurred to me that I may have unwittingly stretched the meaning of Carlos' thinking. After all, I had only heard him talking, not the people at the other end. What if this getting above themselves wasn't about actual plans, but just feeding themselves with high hopes, competing in chest-beating? A little like soccer players before their matches?

Or was it, God forbid, playing to the gallery? Not once

had he lowered his voice. A pageant for me, but why? So I be impressed and take it for more than it is worth? Good enough for his one-third of the capital needed?

Dangerous ground ahead; I was well aware that I should watch my step now. There was a mine of guilty conscience – and what it could stir up I knew all too well.

14

Her spell at Osman Excelsior over, Madeleine took on some work as a back therapist at a newly opened *relaxation resort* between Patara and Kash, with saltwater pools and small-scale imitations of famous landmarks; there was even an Eiffel tower with a Health Café on the first floor.

She appreciated her own 'bird tower' much more, however. On the gable of one of the resort buildings, there was a balcony quite high up, set aside as a smoking area for the staff, where she had rigged her telescope. She visited it whenever she was free. On a little wetland not very far off, she could see herons, spoonbills and some ibis, also ducks that eluded identification.

Since Carlos had been close by, they had been lunching together on and off.

"What of his… paramour?" I asked.

"Paramour? Her name is Elif! As it happens, I asked him."

"Yes?"

"He just gave a giggle. She's nice, that's about all, it appears."

Whether there was more and I wanted to know about it, I do not remember, but suddenly I heard myself saying: "Madeleine, should you have lunch with him again, perhaps you wouldn't mind telling him that it may be rash to believe in wholehearted support on my part for any plans he would feel like pursuing."

Yes, this was fairly exactly how my words came out, and I

remember I was quite pleased with 'wholehearted'. After some moments, she answered.

"But I do mind," she said, looking me straight in my eye. "This is the kind of errand you are best suited to run yourself, yes?"

How foolish of me! I should have realised that myself even before it slipped off my tongue. If nothing else, who wants to be a messenger of bad news?

"Well… I just wanted to make it clear that I don't have any money. Jens has all of it on his hands."

"For one thing, Birger," she replied, turning up her nose – or was it rather something snort-like? I don't remember – "that would be stretching the truth."

"Not figuratively speaking, no."

She continued in a much lower voice:

"Wouldn't Jens cough up any amount you wanted, if you asked him in earnest? Is he in any position to say no to you?"

"It's not as easy as all that."

I gave an inward sigh. I wanted to race away for a few drops of something bracing from the *pressure cooker*.

Not just for a pause. I would gladly get shot of the need to collect my thoughts again. Yes, fed up with this discussion, the more so as I bore the blame for it myself. Besides, my head was feeling heavy, and no wonder as grey clouds were massing over the western ridge; I am sensitive to low air pressure, have been so all my life.

"You know, Jens doesn't necessarily have the money readily available; there are budgets and he would have to make arrangements, you see, to get it from somewhere, in which case, I presume, it would be necessary…" I said, slowly petering out with something I don't recall, of no significance perhaps, until Madeleine gracefully let me off the hook.

"Anyway, all this is beside the point. Money is no problem for them."

"No problem? What do you mean? For Carlos as well?"
"They've got some kind of loan. A 'stopgap'. What's that?"
"Aah!"

I took a deep, deep breath, of the kind I draw only once a year, if that. So it wasn't just bricks without straw. My intuition – all wrong. It had assumed too much. Enough! I would cut its throat, draw it through the smallest of CBT drawing dies!

I think I sighed again, heavily. What a relief, really. I could see off my worries now, at least those for myself. Perhaps there would be a residual one for Carlos and his part of the loans. Or no, not even that. We have to trust banks to know their forte?

Madeleine gave me a broad, friendly smile. Really becoming, her front teeth appearing as white and well shaped as they must have been in her youth and, I guess, during her milk-teeth years too, as far as one could gather from black and white photos taken by her father.

She ought to have perceived both my relief and self-reproach. Perhaps even realised that, quite unnecessarily, I had been haunted by my conscience.

Apart from all his other qualities, Madeleine's father was an accomplished photographer with his own darkroom in the cellar of their old house, Madeleine being one of his most cherished subjects. One photo, my favourite, portrays her on broad wooden skis with leather bindings together with her mother, both in anoraks, peeling oranges and smiling at the camera and the low winter sun, both with the same smile and front teeth. Her father's shadow is in there too. Pinned up on the notice board above my computer, it has long since yellowed. The negative is kept in the trousseau chest her dad made for her first marriage, together with innumerable others, a needle in a haystack.

"They would even be a bit overfunded."

Roused from my reverie, I stuttered:

"What did you just say? Overfunded, was it?"

"Yes, Carlos said they were, a bit."

Though Madeleine might think me nitpicking, I couldn't hold back from asking: "

"Where is the money coming from?"

"No idea."

Just as a shadow on the beach scares a crab back into its dark hole, my dissipated uneasiness dashed back into the murky convolutions it had just left.

Overfunded? Hogwash! Empty boast! Why would creditors give lenders more than they need? So much stronger was my impulse to confer with Jens now, although I no longer had the same compelling reason. It would just have to be on the strength of my natural desire to know. Simple curiosity – or disappointingly, even indignantly so?

15

There was a lot of mail on this hazy day. Documents from Jens, which, whether I read them or not, I will add my signature to or, more to Jens' liking, my name in full, together with materials from Madan Mogra, a few letters and some magazines, all of which were nicely piled up at the reception desk.

Atatürk, in his usual pose, was looking up at the sky, or the stars of the future, but, as paintings go (though this was only a photo reproduction), you could feel his eyes on you, falling on the pile too. On top, there was a note saying Zia wanted to see me.

He came and grasped my right hand, took it between his own, wiry and strong as the rest of him. He was wearing a turquoise short-sleeved shirt, which went strikingly well with his complexion. As more often than not, he was less than well shaven, which is one of our similarities, although our reasons differ; for me, it's the convenience of not doing it; for him, it's the electric shaver blades that have gone dull.

"If you only knew how happy I am for Elif. Just perfect, just perfect for her!"

His lips overflowed with joy, his eyes too, even his comely wrinkles, it seemed and, although puzzled, I decided my top priority should be not to ruin any of it.

I mumbled a little discreetly, rather less brightly than I had meant to.

What was he hinting at? Something he had brought up earlier, I guessed. Something he had told me in passing... bumping into me perhaps when I had just gone out for a breather, mind-defragmentation walk –early on, while I was still unable to download information into my head.

"At the Teachers' Union Hostel, she was working far below her education."

"Aha," I said. "Her education?"

"Didn't you know? The English Commercial School in Mugla, two semesters. With a scholarship from the Municipality."

Perhaps he had told me that also.

"To take care of international guests, that's quite another thing."

I nodded in agreement, but was even more at a loss now.

Ever since my school days, I've been good at putting on an air of innocence in awkward situations. For all I know, classmates were rehearsing toughness à la Steve McQueen in front of their bathroom mirrors, but that was not my way; mildness would do me more good. It was the kind of school where you couldn't admit to weakness of any sort, particularly if, like me, you had got undeservedly high marks. A pity to show Zia this face, but it was for him, not for me.

"How often will you be able to see her?" I asked, chancing it was a reasonable question.

"She will live with us, of course, except some time when she will work late. That's all right, I think. After all, Kash is a bit far off, don't you think?"

Kash?

I made a roundabout walk back to our whitewashed little hamlet following the westernmost track that after a while accompanies one of the streams to the sea. Here and there, high plume grass with trembling panicles gifted to gleam in the sun like gold or silver, and swept copper too, along with various types of visiting tits sporting black moustaches.

I lingered at the old wooden bridge, over to the desolate terraces on the other side, that is now used only once in a while by wayward tourists and the tame white geese that belong to the bougainvillea-adorned house a stone's throw away.

I leaned on the railing, which felt remarkably solid. My nostrils drew in the scent of damp wood, moss and mould. Below flowed a gentle brook, glittering convivially, yet dark as always this time of the day. The kingfisher that lives here, which always livens you up with its blazing plumage, was nowhere to be seen, perhaps at its other favourite post further down. Never mind, it wouldn't have been good enough for me anyway.

Guess as I might – in spite of everything, including the stubborn gnats swarming around me – I could hit on only one reason for Zia's profuse gratitude: a bonanza for Elif to do with Carlos; he and his pals have something going on in Turkey – and much closer than I thought. In Kash.

I couldn't keep it at a distance. All right, if this is his way of stretching his wings, so be it. But what if he plunges into the sea? Well, he can be as stupid as he wants; everyone has his own way of eating yoghurt, as the Turkish saying goes. I wash my hands of it.

I have no responsibility whatsoever, I kept repeating to myself. Not even now with Elif involved, if she is, as financing has been secured.

All right, at most it would be to find out about the conditions of the loans. But how is that done? The last thing I would expect is for Carlos to tell me details of any kind. And I can't ask Zia to find out through Elif, now that he believes I have a hand in it.

If, against all odds, I could find out about it, then what? What are my motives anyway? Is it that I have a hidden agenda, obscure even to myself? Not as easy as that – I can't support an idea I wouldn't believe in. And I don't want to be cavalier about my money; a bit odd, admittedly, since I certainly have been just that many times over. Not this time, though, and it seems to me I have no reason to involve myself in the matter.

16

It was some time after Carlos had departed.

I had been visiting Ankara on some minor errands – follow-up after the cataract surgery, scavenging bookstores – and was now sitting in the spacious Sheraton lobby bar. Despite its bluish extravaganza and live pianist, it was open to the public and, in my blue-grey corduroy trousers from the village market, I felt well qualified to be there, to enjoy a professionally made caffè latte, extra strong at that. While waiting, a young woman, longish skirt and low heels, decent as a Turkish Airlines hostess, approached with a cart carrying foreign newspapers. I took it for granted she was serving hotel clients, but I reciprocated her vague smile in my direction with a big client-like one and snapped up a copy of the *Financial Times* at random, without her voicing any objection.

As a student, I had known it by name, the mouthpiece of capitalist parasites, favourite reading of the City of London and Wall Street. Had I set eyes on it in those days, it would no doubt have aroused my disgust or more.

I pushed my newly purchased books aside; *A Brief History of Time* on top. This was a broadsheet newspaper, a survivor, so to speak. Not only larger than most contemporaries, but also old-school, low-voiced, I concluded. The main headline addressed the EU's relocation of refugees from Syria – *Schengen Agreement*

Under Pressure – and *Hürriyet*, Turkey's biggest newspaper, lying abandoned on the next table, carried a similar headline, the difference in font size being that between the breadth of a thumb and a whole hand.

I decided to like this newspaper – well kempt, spurning both text elephantiasis and picture hysteria. It struck me: following it would perhaps give me an opportunity to beef up my meagre knowledge of economics, thin like Egyptian parchment, and so, for instance, help me get to grips with a phrase like *Goldman Joins Smart Beta ETF Rush*. Was it economic general knowledge to know the meaning of this?

I threw it in my rucksack with a view to becoming a subscriber.

*

Madeleine knit her brows at it. "It stinks! Why is it pink?"

"Obviously, it's coloured," I replied, "but so are the white ones. Insofar as they are white rather than black," I added, chuckling over my wisecrack.

"What is this?" she said, and pulled out a separate publication which had eluded me, although it was both large and thick. "What's it doing here?"

"Well, it's not surprising. Most dailies have supplements on and off."

This one was a four-colour print with a veteran car on the front page. "A motor magazine?" I suggested.

"It's called *How to Spend It*," she said, and started to dip into it. "How much is it, the subscription?"

"No idea," I confessed, "is it important?"

"As I'm the one who pays the bills in this household, I'm curious to know."

We have no problem whatsoever with money, far from it.

"Look," she said, clearly displeased, "a whole page with just one watch, and here is one more, yet another, and… here one with its intestines on show, you can barely see the hands for all the cogwheels and odds and ends. What an idea. What an offensive name: *How to Spend It*."

She agitated herself: "How much is a watch like this? They don't even mention the prices."

"This magazine comes with the newspaper. I can't help it, but it isn't that that I'm going to subscribe to."

She turned back to the front page. "It says *FINANCIAL TIMES*: *How to Spend It*!" And pushed it, quite contentedly it seemed, away from herself.

Admittedly, she had a point. Now, this extra thing, a weekly perhaps, comes with the newspaper and you can't opt out of it. I asserted this without knowing, of course. Anyway, it can't be a touchstone for my subscription, can it?

It occurred to me that Zia might catch a glimpse of it, since this newspaper, like all other items of mail to us, would come to the hotel. What would his reaction be to seeing these watches and the rest? Well, at least he knows that I don't have a wristwatch. As it turned out, he never breathed a word about the newspaper, neither the daily pink thing nor any of its supplements, of which there were several issued rather regularly, and reading it made me quite a bit more knowledgeable. And then, quite unexpectedly, it helped us keep track of Carlos' doings.

Madeleine drew the magazine to her as if to give it a second chance, or, more likely, a second clip.

"What's the meaning of something like this?"

"Advertising, I guess."

She lifted her eyes; more than a glance, less than a stare, though.

"Hey, here they are, the prices," she exclaimed. "*Hublot*

Classic Fusion Extra Slim. Sounds like... like a *trotter*. Guess how much."

"One should guess, as much as a good trotter," I said with a grin. "Ten thousand euros?"

"Tsk, twenty-five thousand! Pounds! Several annual salaries for a Turk! Isn't it outrageous?"

It wasn't a plain rhetorical question, rather a plea for support, which I was far from happy to face.

"What's the meaning of buying a watch that price? Even if you have money to spare? I can't imagine any watch being worth that much."

I was half-thinking of asking *What is the maximum price for a watch anyway?*, but as good as this point was, I opted for something milder: "Can our way of living be the yardstick for others?"

"Why not!"

I offered resistance once more.

"If so, I suppose we'll be bound to formulate some principles, some norms, to underpin our opinions."

There was a silence, rather intrusive. I shifted feet a couple of times but had to break it myself.

"I, for one, have nothing to offer."

In the slime of my subconscious, one or two *principles* might still flounder, but otherwise they strike doubt and jitters into my heart; so little is needed to disturb my mental balance. Besides, regardless of principles or norms, it just happens that watches like these don't appeal to me at all, like most of the other items Madeleine had flicked past, be it crocodile-marked shawls, cufflinks, or whatever.

"My moral aptitude isn't as nimble as it used to be," I said, "only ten years ago."

"Please, lay off these contortionist tricks, I hate them," she replied. "People shouldn't have to guess if you are joking."

I feared she saw me as standing just an inch from one of my staple litanies and hastened to gamble that a radical scene shift would pass.

"Did you know there is a Reader's Queries? That should interest you, on everyday life actually."

Not notably impressed, it appeared, she at least moved her lips a little, if mostly on one side. I moved a few pages back and forth before looking up at her. Yes, a little curious she was, no doubt, so I started reading out, or no, not reading, scanning:

Dear Mrs Query:
It's good to lead a principled life. My wife surely does but I disgracefully fail to match. Yet everyone says we get on well, and so I've thought for twenty-odd years. Is it a genuinely insoluble problem; what do you think?

Madeleine replies, "*Mrs Query would tell you not to over-intellectualise. To beware of your headache and trust your intuition.*"

It took some moments before I felt that our discussion mustn't end like this: intuition as a lodestar instead of principles.

If so, I would have to make a PS to my letter:

Mrs Query, I can't use my intuition, either, since I don't trust it; it varies from one day to the next, not to mention days of acid reflux, yea, already the ancient Greeks knew about this. And then, Mrs Query, it might differ with others' intuition. But that is another story. Isn't it?

We smiled together, hatchet-burying, I thought. That she had joined in the charade was the best part.

17

I had to call there. I had to find out.

We have our little Peugeot parked at the hotel, behind the whitewashed garden wall next to Zia's Turkish-made Fiat and the chef's motorcycle. Any staff member, according to our agreement with the hotel, is free to use it when an extra vehicle is needed, provided they keep it serviced and fill it up, at our expense.

It's our guess they use it far more than we do. Anyhow, there it was, 'Kingfisher blue', as if supplying us with a pet name – clean and without any visible road rash, in spite of all the gravel roads round here. So I headed off towards Kash.

From the driveway that reveals a glass-fronted entrance porch, I caught a glimpse of a young woman standing just inside the doors decorated with a frosted flourish monogram, *E* and *P*, surrounded by abstract greenery. She could well be Zia's daughter – Elif. And the two letters, what did they stand for? *Economic* something?

Whereas the yard was a barren area covered with little but dry grass and parking gravel, there were groups of lush pot plants inside the hexagonal reception hall, the biggest one an imaginatively branching ficus with huge leaves, fiddle-leaf fig, which otherwise belongs in West Africa and in the wild can grow up to 30 metres.

I found Elif at a short counter next to an airy flight of curved stairs – standing erect, formally dressed in dark brown. Undoubtedly a handsome woman, her prettiness was of the kind that comes out best from a distance, as if her mouth and nose become less prominent, and so much more like Carlos, too, I thought.

How proud Zia would be seeing her in this setting.

"Hi," I said.

"Good day," she uttered curtly.

We exchanged perfunctory bows as if forgetting the fact that we were no strangers to each other.

"I've come just to say a brief hallo to Carlos," I said, not giving my name, which she well knew of course, and revenging myself for her part in our silly masquerade. *So the thigh-show is not on today*, I felt tempted to add.

"He is busy till noon," she said, "when he will be taking a large party for lunch."

On the gallery above us, I could see chairs which looked comfortable and said I thought I would sit there a while, then went upstairs without waiting for her answer, if there should be any.

From my lofty position, I could hear the little fountain on the marble floor at reception, the droplet sound rising and falling like a Catholic priest's sing-song, so discreet that I imagined I could hear the motor as well. I produced a book, *Night and Mist*, about the guerrilla war in Southeast Turkey, but couldn't bend my mind to it, and my eyes started to travel around the slightly arched ceiling instead.

For God's sake, what am I sitting here for? Is this typical behaviour, or is it not? Setting out without a defined purpose and before I know it, trapping myself in this odd situation. How did it happen? As if choosing a curved line, even when the straight line is readily available.

Bending forward a little, I could look down a long, shiny parquet corridor leading out from where I was sitting. The bright daylight was flowing in through a balcony door at the end.

A man was approaching with jaunty, yet not quick, strides. A bit on the stocky side. As he came closer, I noted he was chewing something rather resolutely, if you see what I mean. Chewing gum, of course, which wasn't very becoming. His face was a landscape of rather big proportions and now everything was shaken by eruptions. Noticing me, at just a few metres away, everything stopped at once. He gave his name as Terry and extended his hand.

"Birger," I said, and made an effort to rise, but he signalled in a friendly arm gesture to remain seated in my leather-woven lounge chair. Most likely this was one of Carlos' two companions, although I didn't recall the names which I had come across in my google reconnaissance. Anyhow, he must be the Egyptian or else the South African, probably the former; his hair and mouth were as Arab as Arab can be. In all likelihood, he was acting on a message from Elif, I thought, seeing that his left hand was clasping a mobile. Yes, he probably was, but as for his identity I was mistaken, as I later learned that he was the South African, whose father, by the way, was of Greek extraction.

"What an elegant front door," I said, "a work of art, these letters E and P..."

I made a brief pause for him to, hopefully, tell me their meaning.

"*Executive Paladin*," he said with a faint smile.

"Ah. And the intertwined vines, beautiful."

"Thank you so much. We were very lucky to contract a calligraphy master from Delhi to do it."

"Is that right?"

"Yes, and if you take a closer look," he continued, still smiling, and tilting his head slightly to one side, "you can see intertwined serpents, which is an ancient oriental symbol."

"Aha," I replied, nothing more, as I was a bit perplexed. If memory served me well, the Paladin was some kind of European medieval knight. And the vines, which in reality were a snake's nest, an oriental symbol. What did it all add up to? Unless I asked him, I wouldn't understand, and yet I held my breath so he wouldn't expand on it.

"Carlos is giving an introductory talk right now, one of our most novel and important sessions."

"Oh, I wouldn't disturb him. What is it about?"

"It's a computer simulation. The students will be engaged in asset handling. In stressed market environments."

'Stress' crossed my mind. Would this computer- stressing thing possibly be one of their *thermometers*?

"Go and take a look, if you wish, the door is open," he said, and pointed towards a second corridor further away.

I rose to my feet, rather glad to be relieved of this conversation.

The door was at the back of the simulation hall and I could easily see rows of people of both sexes, fairly smartly dressed, although not so comfortably, perhaps, given that there were one or two with their ties pulled down, who sat listening behind green computer desks.

"You will presently get your personal passwords."

It was Carlos speaking.

For a while, I just stood listening to his voice. Astounded. It was as agreeable as a *viola da gamba* with its mellow tone, but a bit subdued. He could easily be chanting in some dignified place such as the Blue Mosque in Istanbul, all the more mystifying then that his telephone voice was rather that of a mass-produced violin, fresh from the factory, harsh and constructed primarily to be heard.

As I couldn't see him, I poked my head little by little around the doorpost.

He was in the middle of drawing a huge diagram on a white board, lines running back and forth between boxes of varying sizes, with labels and texts that I couldn't read.

"In fact," he said – I am paraphrasing – "we repeat *actual situations*, just that names of market actors, sellers and buyers, have been altered, as have dates. And, of course, the *time perspective*, for effectiveness, *has been compressed*."

He was talking in a slightly more eager voice now, accompanying himself with arms and hands; he had come to life as I had never seen him, at least not for many, many years. In his early teens perhaps; Carlos, barefoot with swinging arms, enthusiastically marching to the fridge for a Coke, victoriously shutting himself up with his computer games again. No, now I'm being unfair to him, so let that be unsaid.

"Note that when you open the program, you will be all on your own and all of you have been given different circumstances. Remember, it's up to you to decide whether the information you will receive is of no account or something to act on. *Rather like a blind date, don't you think?*"

There was laughter and clapping of hands. How come, uncommunicative that he is, he knows how to work an audience?

I felt uncomfortable and turned away. As I passed in front of Carlos' colleague, Terry, still on the landing, reading his mobile, he started to rise.

If not endowed with an attractive outer appearance, he was certainly a man of courteous manners, I thought, and tried to emulate his gesture from five minutes earlier. "Interesting," I said, "really interesting. Well, I was just driving by and needed a break, and now I am fully restored." I reached out my hand: "No need to tell him I popped in."

Where on earth did I get that from?

Saying things spontaneously is getting harder and harder these days. Takes me such a long time to think things out, and, if I don't, stupidities follow, like *streptococcus* bacteria chains.

Not until I was seated behind the steering wheel could I fully recover my breath. I opened the windows but shut off the engine again, just for a moment. A slight breeze blew in. A big black car, dwarfing mine, SUV-like and sporting the *Executive Paladin* logo on its front door was parked next to mine now.

Most of what Carlos had been saying was beyond me.

But it had dawned on me that he might possess some gravitational momentum after all, as a speaker; a fine item to put on his balance sheet – if I dared use a term picked up from the *Financial Times*. Maybe, when in a computer room he is at his best?

Telling Madeleine so: would it be a dumb thing to do or would it gladden her heart?

18

"Hello, I am the Administrative Assistant at Executive Paladin. We met briefly some time ago."

Her voice was higher than I remembered it, having switched from alto to mezzo.

"Yes?"

"I hope I'm not disturbing you?"

What on earth could she want?

I was puzzled, not only that she should have something to talk about, but even more that she should have this mobile number. Not many knew it. Madeleine of course; otherwise, it was my hotline to Jens.

"You see, I have a tricky task to carry out… and I just wanted to know if you could possibly assist me in finding a missing person. He is a Ukrainian businessman who is scheduled to be here at the Paladin but isn't, and has left us without leaving any message. It's all a bit… delicate, as we don't know what has happened to him…"

Oh, there's a nice girl, and how come, I thought, giving an internal laugh which faltered as a sudden wonder took over.

"Is Carlos on it?"

"Well, at the moment, he is busy monitoring an important session. Unfortunately, this is a rather urgent matter that I don't know if I can handle alone."

Zia had every reason to be proud of his daughter, just as much of her drive as her English, and I wouldn't forget to tell him. Some moments elapsed without a word being uttered on either side, until I, vainly trying to consider her request in a sensible way, put an end to it: "I'll be there, hopefully within half an hour."

As I knew the road now it didn't take long, but it has to be said that I stepped on it whenever it was possible. Doing so, I learned that my spirited red bug was equipped with a booster or something; as soon as it got into the 100s, it suddenly leapt forward like a scared horse.

I could well give Elif a hand, I told myself, sitting fiddling with the many gears, one more than normal it seemed. Why not? She is a nice girl in her heart of hearts; I'm my own master, nothing pressing right now apart from some delayed responses to Jens on some investment ideas. "Okay with me, just go ahead." Real estate in Copenhagen and the Baltic. The more scrupulous he is about my approval, the laxer my attitude.

When I pulled up at the main entrance, she came running out straight away, and this time she gave me a handshake through the car window, unexpectedly clammy. Otherwise, she was as elegant as last time, well, perhaps a little more simply dressed.

She handed me a car key.

"We had better take that one," she said, pointing towards the parking lot and a van singling itself out by its breadth and length, dwarfing my Peugeot by a factor of two, if not three.

"So, you have two cars?"

"Yes, sometimes more, on lease."

"And you have no driving licence?"

"Well, I have…"

When I turned my head towards her, she said: "But I can't drive."

This car had an impressive dashboard. Horn of plenty. I

opted for a pragmatic approach: least possible fuss getting into it.

"How long will it take to Kash?"

"Oh, it depends very much on the time of the day," she said. "And I have never gone there at this hour."

As the car made a flying start, I concluded: "That makes about seventeen and a half minutes then?"

She gave me a brief glance, caught my grin and erupted – rather like Claudia Cardinale in this film on Sicily in the 1860s, *The Leopard*, like a horse rather than a donkey. How I liked it. Humour can tear down walls, it's said. (No doubt it can be risky too, tearing down bridges, as I have learned over the years.)

This man, a Mr Kulik, had left the campus just like that, without leaving any message whatsoever, but it was a fair guess he had taken a taxi to Kash, which was the nearest seaside resort. Elif produced a little notebook with a soft cover that was full of jotted-down hotel phone numbers, and now she started dealing with them one after another in a very organised and clear way. Every now and then, I couldn't hold back a furtive glance; her complexion lighter than Zia's, not just a shade, probably coming more from her mother, a brunette from Edirne on the European side, close to Greece. I couldn't see the need for her eyeliner.

As we descended the last stretch of the serpentine road down into Kash, Elif had just found out that Kulik had gone to the Hotel Naxos.

"He shouldn't have done it," she said. "We have a contract with the participants and there is no exception clause in his case. He has been sitting in the bar, drinking beer after beer, washing it down with *raki*."

Elif left the hotel after less than one minute. For an hour he had been there, but then said he would go on to a *superior* place, *Mediterranean*, further down the street with a bigger pool, displeased with the service, not forthcoming enough. "They didn't specify. I guess he's just a cantankerous person."

Cantankerous? Is that why she called me?

"Couldn't Carlos have done this?" I asked, incredulous that he wouldn't have broad enough shoulders.

"He might have done it, perhaps, if the car had been ready in time. Before the meeting."

Sounded less than crystal clear to me. Anyway, you can always get a taxi from somewhere, can't you? Or was this a mission too sensitive for a taxi to be involved? And why me? Was it that Elif counted on my friendship with Zia?

"Did you say it was a delicate matter?"

"He is from a well-known bank in Kiev. And Kash…"

She didn't finish her sentence but I think I understood; they had to protect their good name here and an important customer had sent him. She had put her hands in her lap now, fingers twisted together. Whether this had any special meaning in Turkish culture, I didn't know; otherwise, it might have been taken as embarrassment.

I felt something unwanted hovering on my mind's threshold – deception – or one of its close relatives. But I decided to send it packing. To the best of my knowledge, no blame could be laid at Elif's door for this.

There was a big, shiny lobby. With a hazy copy of a passport photo depicting a man of rather ordinary appearance in her hand, Elif approached the front desk decisively. The first glance was enough for the grizzled receptionist: "Yes, I guess he's still in the pool," he said, void of expression.

And there he was, Mr Kulik, in the middle of a spacious kidney-shaped pool. Quite obese – and well afloat, for the same reason.

His face was ruddy with freckles, or just spotted in other ways, including some white patches; vitiligo. You couldn't see much of his eyes, which were somehow embedded, plum-studded-like, unless he had just fallen asleep out there. He wasn't moving. I imagined a whale entangled in sargassum seaweed would look like that; in fact, this whale fish was enmeshed in something –something white, and now it started gesticulating weakly with its fins to try to fend it off.

The whole picture, truly bizarre, would have caught the imagination of a surrealist, an absurd *oeuvre* by Dali's hand. Or Picasso's *Guernica*.

Several hotel staff of dignified bearing were posted around the kidney and told us they were prepared to grab him in case he came near the rim (without any observable alacrity, though). He had been shouting and singing in Russian, or Ukrainian, no one knew for sure which it was, chasing away the guests. My eyesight not what it used to be, I asked:

"What's the white mess around him?"

"Is it plaster?" Elif suggested.

"Plaster?"

I have seen lots of people in orthopaedic casts up to their knees but certainly never seen them bathing.

"Is he injured?"

"Not that I know."

I took off my shirt, trousers and sandals and jumped in, in the hope of appealing to his sense of reason, fair play or conscience. I, treading water at some metres' distance, started to talk to him: "Are you all right? Would you like me to…" No answer from him, other than, as far as I could guess, a series of expletives. I attacked him fore and aft, grabbed the belt on his Bermuda shorts and started hauling, feeling rather energised by this opportunity to use my physical power. Without mishap, he was towed to the shallow part of the pool, to the rim, where the hotel people landed him.

I paid a handsome sum of money for their stoical qualities, and also for their silence of course.

Until our whale fish had been bundled into the back seat on some hotel towels, I had been acting more or less on instinct. Now, driving back, it was high time for reflections. I didn't refrain from sharing one or two of them with Elif, who was sitting with me and certainly not keen on being in the back watching over our passenger, if nothing else because he was soaking everything around him.

"Some of their... of the *Paladine* ideas, may be sound," I said in Turkish, before pausing a little, "but this joystick handling of it gives me the creeps."

She hadn't really anything to share with me but at least smiled vaguely. Something like the air of a marathon winner, happy but tired.

Time and again, she turned round to the back seat. Each time her dress came up a little so that she finally got tired of drawing it down again. No doubt about it, she took her mission seriously. I couldn't keep my mouth from saying aloud:

"Pretty complicated method this."

"What do you mean?"

"Putting a sinker on people," I said in Turkish, knowingly and not without a certain mirth.

"Well, I assume they wanted to do an extra test on him."

That she cared to answer made me glad, the more so as she seemed to understand my thoughts.

"Usually, crapulence is something you can easily sniff out. Without plaster, so to speak," I added, no doubt with my hilarity growing larger still.

And she reciprocated – a smile as generous as a smile can be without one's teeth taking part in it.

The day was fairly advanced when we reached the 'Paladin Academy', or whatever the proper name for it was.

This should be a windy place up here, I thought. Wuthering Heights. Not all days, though, not today, nor the last time.

I helped Elif to get our passenger, who had completely run out of steam now, to his room, and then lingered in the entrance hall for a while in case Carlos might turn up. The huge fiddle-leaf fig was gone, having made room for a wrought iron sofa, which, besides being practical –guests could sit down there like nesting in a mini-garden – was a truly decorative piece in its rounded design. Under the staircase there was a folded-away wheelchair.

19

Carlos came bouncing down the curved stairs, which trembled and rang beneath his feet, one hand clenched over the other, a pastille or something flicking around in his mouth.

"Order restored, I hear."

He stopped in front of us and started massaging his hands the way Turkish restaurant guests do when getting cologne from the waiter on leaving: "Good, very good!"

Was this in lieu of saying thank you? I wondered, instead of saying so outright, which I definitely would have preferred. It had indeed ended well but could easily have ended badly. Say the hotel had called the police, what then? Or what if journalists had got wind of it?

"Is there anything else I can do?" I asked. And prompted by a fleeting urge to make it longer, added: "To help you?"

"Why do you ask that?" The pastille, starkly green, came to light on his lower lip.

No answer occurred to me at first. This was a counter-question as unexpected as it was uncomfortable, Elif's presence adding to its awkwardness.

"Well, there is no *why*. It's quite natural, I should think, that your mother and I, that we—"

Unceremoniously, he cut me off.

"I've always been sensitive to people who come and offer me

a hand with an agenda that I can't see through."

He said this like it was a natural thing to say, almost pro forma; he didn't narrow his eyes or anything.

"Agenda? There's nothing of the kind."

"You've just tried to play the false family card on me."

"What a bunch of baloney, there's no agenda," I repeated, no doubt a little piqued about it. While trying to separate in my mind the wheat of reason from the chaff of irritation, Carlos continued:

"Why do you go around telling people I'm your son?"

"I don't."

"I've heard it myself."

"Who from? Me?"

"You know full well I did."

I pondered this as quickly as I could.

"Oh, when Zia was waiting for us, is that it?"

The nail on the head, probably, as he gave no reaction.

"But that, Carlos, that was just a metaphor, the *Prodigal Son*, a figure of speech!"

"What difference does it make?"

As the long-lived pastille had moved away from his lower lip, the size of a lentil now, he spoke as if bothered by an ill-fitting prosthesis.

I don't remember my reply; I was poised on a knife's edge. If anything, I drew up my shoulders, which certainly didn't prove helpful in finding an answer. Anything seemed open to misunderstanding.

"Shall we take a breath of air and discuss this further?" I suggested, and smiled into his face, admittedly without finesse. We headed for the parking area and a minor road towards the west, went round the back of several long buildings, with grass and trees between them and an open area in front. On the whole, this place was suggestive of an old army barracks, although deftly recast with a boutique-hotel entrance attached to the main building, or, had it been located in northern Europe, a high school from the infancy of the labour or temperance movements.

A thin curtain of shimmering raindrops seemed to be coming towards us, a scene that would have made you stay your steps on any day other than this. Close to sundown as it was, little more than half an hour, we needed time to get back on speaking terms.

Just outside the precinct, about where the sapling plantations start on one side of the road and the coffee bushes on the other, I said, casual and friendly to the best of my ability:

"Your finances all right? We never talked about it."

I wanted perfect intonation but that's not so easy; you must be on top of your air pressure, without any room for hesitation.

"Never talked about it?" There was an edge to his words. "You suppose I can't read your body language?"

Was this his gambit? His brown eyes were staring intensely at me, his brows perfectly wrinkled to match. He wanted to come down on me, that's for sure. I had meant to humour him. In an instant, he was on me again.

"I can tell you it's seldom you meet with such outspoken body language from a highly educated person. A textbook case of squirming like a worm."

"I shouldn't go by that alone," I said, quite upset of course. Presently adding: "Most people take their cues from what you do, rather than what—"

Once more, he cut me off.

"There's always a gap between what people say and what they do. Sure. But" – he spoke jerkily and quickly – "not between what you think and what your outside says. Roars!"

I was flummoxed, or cornered, but far from willing to subscribe to his words, and lapsed into silence.

In my younger climber days, I had practised a certain

countenance taming for some situations in the work place, standard situations, as it were, and so I had *honest commitment* (to my hospital), *genuine interest* (in my colleagues' doings), *general willingness* and a few more poses ready to hand when needed. What my face was like beyond my working environment, I didn't much care about.

Okay, if Carlos finds me readable, that's rather to my advantage, and far more than what can be said about him. This upper-lip curl of his – neither fish nor fowl…

"When I first arrived in Turkey, my very first day, I paid you a compliment: 'nice to hear, Birger, you have been so successful,' I said. And your face instantly dried into a sultana. On top of that, you flatly denied it."

"I haven't been successful. It's not what *I* have done. The long arm of coincidence did it all for me."

"Yea, there you go again."

Indeed, I had explained that my prosperity came from my exploits and that these would have come to nothing had Madeleine and our Danish friend, Jens, not taken them in hand. Carlos, if he had not believed me, could easily have checked it out with Madeleine.

We walked on. The setting sun was right in front of us, a fine rain falling, but I noted gratefully that there was still enough hair on my head for it not to bother me. Usually, Carlos has a carefree gait, but he was walking now like a soldier in combat boots and with a heavy backpack. There was no pavement, so we walked two abreast on the road until a car came towards us and I lagged behind for a moment. Every now and then, we fell into step with each other.

Perhaps this was too much for him; it was on one such occasion that it happened:

"I never asked," he said, "for you to barge in as a *paterfamilias* where I had my home."

I was caught flat-footed – to the degree that several seconds passed before I had taken in his message.

I couldn't believe my ears. *Barged in!* How offensive. Nine on the Richter scale! Stupid. Against his better judgement! And meaning what? That I brought problems on his head; that I stood in his way; that… so in the story of his life, I would go down as the one who had ruined his reputation, spoiled everything, even caused this incident with this Ukrainian?

I felt my cheeks flaming red, as Carlos would have seen if he had just given me a glance, which he failed to. I couldn't help stroking my face; was this Madeleine's fried bacon? The absurdity of it all cooled me down a little. Or was it rather my instinct that he wasn't to be taken seriously that acted on me?

I knew it would be a mistake to trade barbs with him. But damn it, it wasn't going to be a losing battle.

"*Barged in?*" I said, and continued a little tentatively, but not for long. I can't tell what note there was in my voice; I had the idea of not having one, indicative of neither mollification nor aggression, of nothing, my lips barely moving.

"Yea, that's just the way it goes in this world for the very young. Even if you had lodged a protest at the time, you would have been let down. Not even the Convention on the Rights of the Child gives three-year- olds – you were three and a half, I remember – rights vis-à-vis the custodial parent. Yes, the grown-ups are extremely privileged in human rights law – even have the right to start a family at their discretion.

"Can you believe it, even bring a child into the world as they wish," I added, incidentally giving voice to an undigested thought from my student years and getting so carried away by my own words that I almost felt a tinge of nostalgia.

In his eyes, I may have been teetering on the edge of decency. Well, so be it; he had set the rules of the game. Should more be expected of me than him? Fair enough, some might say, as

I have more years and experience of life. Well then, therefore, more capacity to be hurt.

If what I had said wasn't enough, then, dammit, I would certainly cap it off with... I didn't know what. It all ended in silence.

We came to a standstill at a crossroads, but had certainly walked for long enough. The rain had ceased, transforming into a fragrant freshness. Within minutes, the disc that was the sun, which had turned orange above the spruce firs on the other side of the large field, would be gone. A dark bird was sitting in one of the treetops, motionless; rough tractor sounds were coming from somewhere behind.

Carlos lit a cigarette. I didn't know he was a smoker; if he truly was, perhaps a social smoker only, although I wouldn't consider this a social event, certainly not a party. More like a burial.

Giving him furtive glances, while moving in half-circles in front of him, I tried to keep a stiff upper lip as best I could, like being on duty in a danger zone. Surely, with hunched shoulders again.

There was a swarming of agitated thoughts in my head, but what use did I have for them? Whether or not he gave me a glance, I don't know, his eyes seemingly riveted on the ground, not asphalt now, but gravel.

It was futile to continue our discussion, so let it be buried behind the crashed-into signpost standing where the road split. It was bent in several places but still got the directions right all the same; Mugla to the right, Antalya to the left.

Carlos ground the cigarette under his thin leather shoe. Ah, at last, I sighed to myself, let's go. But no, he lit another one. Stoically, I didn't say a word until he gave a sign – a grunt, as it happened – that he was ready to turn back.

There was no moon, only starlight and then, of course, the

lights from the cars. Meeting one was a great nuisance to me (as for anyone who has undergone cataract surgery), but seemingly not for Carlos, who was constantly ahead of me now and walking with confident steps.

Sometimes in stressful situations, the lower part of my body takes command. Engaging the gluteal muscles can steady your balance, knitting toes less so, and there I was stumbling along with toes knitted, and couldn't get myself out of it.

I knew there were holes underfoot, as we were walking on the same roadside now on our way back. I would have rather followed the other side but hesitated to bring it up, out of spirit or at the risk of sparking further rancour. His squared back convinced me. All my misdeeds might not yet have been ticked off; any pretext could be enough for him to ride roughshod over me again.

How long had all this been seething within him? How could I know? There were so many gaps to fill in about him, not least about his gap years. Ugh! I almost shuddered at my unintentional pun.

Was this rancour the real stuff, or just putting on an act? But post-stress reaction was equally possible, since he had every reason to feel distraught on account of this boozer making a spectacle of himself. How facile to take it out on me. But whereas one single attack would have done the trick, he charged at me repeatedly, swallowed up by his own wrath – at least three times, perhaps more. I could no longer separate his outbursts.

A little less tumult in my grey matter now, but little consolation as my stress headache had come to visit, thudding about, only to be expected, really. Did he take it amiss that I had offered my further services – in Elif's presence at that? As if I doubted he had matters in hand? Which I did, and rightly so. But the reason I asked him, tongue in cheek, was that I resented his nonchalance in not thanking me, his ersatz thank you!

I had already had a guilt trip on his behalf over his funding, but one thing was sure: no more such now, thank you very much. In lieu of a guilty conscience, flowers.

*

A pity we had never talked about our relationship; far worse to do it in this unedifying way, both equally ill-tempered. No, not equally. He wanted to draw blood; I congratulate myself on not getting carried away.

And now? Pinning faith on suppression – Clean Slating, Time the Great Healer. What more could be done?

I wouldn't like this leaven to work on Madeleine's conscience. *Would you believe it, Madeleine: when we moved in together, I intruded upon you. That's Carlos' view, you know.* I wouldn't bring it up with her, and reckoned on him doing the same.

When I first moved into her lodgings, it was at her initiative, not mine. Equally merry and resolute, she offered me a drawer in the chest that stood in her bedroom, for practical reasons, so that I wouldn't have to go back to my place to change clothes so often, but I, playing it safe, contented myself with half of it, until a creeping expansion began – or not so creeping after some time, exponential covers it. I have a strong memory of Carlos' delight at having his wrestling buddy so close at hand.

So he picked the wrong bone there.

He might have mixed it up with our visit to the school psychologist. At the time, he wasn't protesting at all; on the contrary, he went with us willingly, but later, under who knows what influences, he may have begun to remember that visit, along with much else, as somehow abusive, concomitantly making a mortification hotchpotch of it all.

Idle thoughts? Yes, indeed, and there were many more of them besides.

Carlos might well have thought me the main mover in contacting the psychologist, and, if so, might not have been wide of the mark. Perhaps, who knows? I for one don't remember, and I'm sure he doesn't, either.

Now, if he regards me as the villain of the piece, what does he want? A sincere apology? Something like the US Congress wanted from Bill Clinton? Or reparations? No, I won't do that, either; and besides, I doubt the wisdom of it.

But who says he wants something – other than the pleasure of spitting it all out? Well, he got that, unless it ruined everything when I pulled the rug from under his feet with my killjoy human rights talk. I hope it did! At least it shut his mouth.

20

We had lived here several years without ever watching a Turkish soap opera – which are hugely popular not only here but all over the Middle East and sometimes even beyond. A big industry, in fact. Now Fatosh, Madeleine's best friend, a good-humoured lady in her mid-forties, beautiful olive complexion, if a little pimpled, had invited us together with some other neighbours to watch a few episodes from an 'unusually good' series, *All in Pieces*, to inaugurate their new television. We leapt at the chance; she is strong-willed too.

For a house in our outpost, her home is very spacious, with a living room almost double the size of ours. The furniture is a mix of European and Turkish. Many pieces have entered Fatosh's world in flat boxes, and the floor is covered by Anatolian carpets with decorative geometric motifs. What above all catches your eye, however, is the *screen*, rigged on a slim stand, huge and slightly curved; we never saw anything as big in an ordinary home.

The invited neighbours are well known to us, as is her easy-going brother, cheerful and stately, an excellent adornment to his own jumbo tractor, and Fatosh's favourite aunt, thin and hair-bunned, who is about our age, but not the handful of other relatives. Madeleine and I sit down on an IKEA sofa bed together with her aunt between us, whereas the others take seats on cushions on the floor. Presently, a wave of children of all ages show up from nowhere, although in a surprisingly orderly fashion, to fill the remaining gaps.

Fatosh gave us a résumé of the first thirty-something episodes, brief presentations of the protagonists, quite a lot, and some minor characters, who are even more numerous, as they should be, of course, all with tangled relations, always in Istanbul. Then she switched on the screen.

We dropped down right into a profusion of love's endearments, kisses mostly of an innocent kind, but very quickly there was equally as much hostility (cum smashing of glass), all of it simmering in a casserole dish of secrecy, lies and conspirations – a crisis about every quarter of an hour, peppered with atmospheric music.

Whenever needed, Fatosh glided over to the IKEA honorary loge with detailed explications, not just for Madeleine and myself, but for all of us – five now with Fatosh's two crew-cut boys sitting on the sofa's armrests. Well needed, as the story was a bit too quick for both us and her aunt.

If the plot was complicated, so much simpler was the moral take on things, and there arose a wonderful chatter in the audience, like during the silent film era, I imagine.

We unanimously closed ranks behind the well-behaved teenage girl against the well-heeled, chilly mother (who turned out to be only a foster mother) and behind her biological mother, beautiful Gülseren, or *Joyous*, poor and trampled, who had unknowingly reared a different girl, a disgrace, who in fact was the true daughter of the chilly mother. Most of all we were on the side of Elvis-haired Cihan, whatever troubles he was meeting, admittedly virtuous enough to do without our support but, alas, married to the chilly mother. Oh, let him divorce Chilly and have pitiable Joyous once her jailbird spouse has set her free.

Three episodes, then a break; time for a smoke outside for

some, and *dolmas* and filo rolls filled with spinach for others, as well as nuts, juice and *raki* served from a table with legs chubby like an Ardennes horse's, and lively discussion for all: *That terrible daughter is like her true mother to a T, don't you think? Same nastiness in her voice! Why Joyous can't dump her? Yes, and she would be fine if only Elvis...*

Madeleine and I preferred to talk to Fatosh's hair-bun aunt, Serpil. She was married to a Turkish former diplomat and had lived in many countries all over the world, her best memories from Spain, her worst from Saudi Arabia, where she had been shut up for three years with two little twins and a maid in a stuffy house in Riyadh. She would never reconcile herself to wearing *abaya* or *niqab*: "I cried with joy whenever we could get to Turkey for a holiday," she said with a melancholy eye, flitting her long-sleeved shirt-clad arms about.

I tried to drag it out as long as possible, lest Captain, in agony about his big toe, would catch me; some hereabouts see me as a find, always at their service. His toe is bright red and adorned with a green nail, and he believes it's putrefying; *Birger, don't you feel the smell?* (I can only smell his cologne.)

No, no, it's just a fungal infection, tinea, nothing serious, and most people don't care about it. But he has his doubts. It's sometimes called *athlete's foot*, I say, which doesn't cheer him up. If he ever was an athlete, he is innumerable sweet *baklavas* beyond that now.

The second half, only two episodes, offered fresh intricacies, although in the same casserole. Strong feelings, crockery on the floor... enlivening indeed, but our staying power was running out. Elvis, never mind his virtue, was a strain on us, his voice too thick, and that of Chilly's lover yet thicker, in particular when he was at his vilest.

All the guests said goodbye at the same time in front of the mound of shoes in the hall. A big kissing feast. Next week again

– for those who want to come! *You see, Elvis meets a new lady, a female kickboxer! And for Cansu…* We missed hearing about her, the well-behaved girl, and I was already contemplating on what pretext I could excuse myself.

I had to run it off and followed one of my favourite routes along the hollow behind the hotel to a signpost quite high up. The trail is broad and curved in such a way that there's no need to use headlamps as long as the sky is clear and studded with bright stars.

Not surprisingly, next morning, I had to pay tribute to my superego, which sent me headache and heartburn, a minimal silver lining being that I ate my breakfast slowly as dyspepsia patients are strictly advised to do. So stupid to be enticed by the *joie de vivre* into drinking *raki*. Madeleine didn't. However, I had to cheer up; after all, there was a deadline for the manuscripts I had precipitately taken it upon myself to review for the *Journal of War Dermatology*. Hadn't I made a promise last New Year's Day not to get involved in deadlines anymore?

It was then that the house telephone rang.

Unwilling as I was to pick up the receiver, I did it anyway, as Jens' calls are always important, at least for him, and this time I had been notified that he wanted to discuss agenda items over the phone for an upcoming board meeting that I would not be attending. Might as well get it out of the way.

I had already begun to imagine him standing in front of me, with a broad smile you would guess at rather than perceive under his beard, and to wonder whether I might ask to call back in a couple of minutes with a coffee at hand.

But it was Elif.

"I just wanted to speak with you," she said, her voice a bit breathy. "It was such an abrupt end to our expedition."

"Well, yes. I guess it was."

"I understand that Carlos lashed out at you and all I wanted to say is that I'm really sorry about that, and also that I'm very grateful for your help."

It took me a few moments to collect myself. *All in Pieces*, I thought, my own soap opera, second episode, and now *Joyous* is calling me.

"I'm glad. We did a good job, really."

What else could I say? "Let's draw a line under the rest," I suggested, as brightly as I could.

"Thank you," she said. "Unfortunately, I feel I am to blame for it all."

"Really, how do you mean?"

"I should have consulted him, that at least."

Although eager to know more – consulting Carlos before calling me in, was that it? – I wouldn't pursue it, just thanked her again for calling me. Her voice had felt a little pressed, as if she had been calling from an old-fashioned telephone booth – warm, narrow and stuffy but without true privacy, as I remember them. During our escapade, it had been an ordinary, clear young-lady voice.

I wasn't sure why Carlos had jumped on me but now a new idea came to me: he couldn't reconcile himself to the thought – no, no, to the *fact* – that I had been a witness to a cringeworthy event. Even worse, I had been the one to clear it up. But this thought brought another in its wake. Elif could have tipped me off? Or could she not?

Ugh! I would be much better off if thoughts like these were routed out of my mind, and so I laced on my trekking shoes to do an encore of yesterday's trip and on a sudden impulse snatched my running backpack from the hall rack, in case I came across cans or other waste, as I tended to without fail. But once outside the house, I changed my mind, and pulled out the mountain bike from the garden shed. This glimmering vehicle is more seldom used than the wheelbarrow, ladder and lawnmower that were barring the way.

I would challenge myself up in the mountains. Yes, starting from the narrow terraces that had lain deserted since God knows when, I would see how far I could climb at the steepest point. That was my last thought before I zoomed away. Madeleine didn't notice me leaving the house – thankfully, as I was not wearing my red helmet.

21

"I had lunch with Carlos yesterday at the Buyuk Hotel," Madeleine said casually.

"You did? How was it?"

"I had just finished my morning sessions and was relaxing with a cappuccino at the bar outside when he popped up. Driving a huge car."

"Aha, black, with an intricate logo on the front doors, perhaps," I said, unable to come up with anything better. She gave a vague nod.

"Could be, yes. He told me you had met recently."

"Well, yes, we did – the same day that you set out for the Buyuk, I think. But this Tarzan-framed co-worker picked you up in the afternoon, didn't he? So, the day after, then."

These had been drizzly days and the kitchen windows were striped. Our car, currently parked outside the house, was stained too, but marmoreal rather than striped. We had carried down some bushes from the mountain and stone for a rockery in the garden, many dusty trips. To be honest, the back is far from developed, at most, a garden-to-be.

"I don't think your recommendations to him went down too well," Madeleine said.

"Recommendations? I don't know about that." My God, is this going to be my own *All in Pieces III*? "The thing is, Elif called me to ask me to give her a hand."

"Elif? How does she come into this?"

"For one thing, she's working with them."

"She works there?"

"Didn't you know?"

Neither I nor Carlos, I had taken as a given, would breathe a word about our showdown. But our relationship was certainly not built on trust, and he has obviously loosened his tongue. Well now, what about my story?

"Remember when Carlos first arrived?" I said. "At the hotel, I told Zia the parable of the *Prodigal Son*."

"Yes, you did, and it came as no surprise that Zia didn't follow. You could as soon expect him to understand *Get thee to a nunnery*."

"What's that?"

"Shakespeare, I think. Funny you don't know."

"All right, I agree, foolish of me. Now it turned out that Carlos misunderstood it too."

"Why should you expect anything else? He reads manuals, not the Holy Writ."

"Any European language is full to the brim with *winged words* from the Bible, whether we recognise their origin or not. Anyway, there was no need for him to tell me off like a schoolboy." I said it peevishly. Come to think of it, if Carlos had known this expression was from the Bible, he could have used it against me: all right, I'm the prodigal son, so open your arms and your wallet too, no conditions, please.

"Now you are exaggerating."

"No, not at all. He said… Anyway, he gave me a telling-off for that, and then I offered him my services and got another one for that. Believe me, there was certainly a sting in what he said."

In his rancour vespiary was on the tip of my tongue.

"So you put him down, did you?" she said, and looked me over in a surprisingly calm way.

"I wrong-footed him, as simple as that."

It hadn't been simple at all. I was repeatedly walloped, and of all the injuries suffered he picked last the one of my *intrusion into his family*. Was that the smell of pure spite or wasn't it? And an adequate riposte – should it be in kind or with mockery?

Madeleine gave a little smile, although there was something taut about it. Otherwise, her aspect was as well-being as well-being could be, more filled-out than for a long time, and a Vitamin D+ kind of skin; she had definitively subdued her eczema now. I would of course have preferred her to give me an approving nod. She believes the best of him quite naturally, sees him rather as a rough diamond, I guess. Uncut indeed, but diamond?

My discomfort, or worse, from when he emptied his vessel of wrath over me, returned now. How I wanted to speak my mind: we've always thought of him as a bit retired, withdrawn, haven't we? And yes, he was – as retired as a sniper! He may have thought we were on his home turf, where taking liberties is all right? But I was invited there, not trespassing, and had been useful. A well-chosen moment to open fire! And, believe me, I never saw him uglifying his face in that way even in his teenage years, almost dared not look at him lest I should see the corners of his mouth frothing.

It would have been fine to find out together with Madeleine how his mind works, but this was impossible, unless I told her how he had crowned it all: *intruder*! A hair's breadth from saying: but for you, I would have had an excellent childhood, a fantastic youth, and this damned Ukrainian alcoholic wouldn't have disgraced me, either.

"Was it really necessary," she sighed, "quarrelling? Can't you go the extra mile, build a bridge?"

"He may feel he doesn't need a bridge. And even accused me of… ", I said, waiting for the rest of it to tumble out all by itself so that somehow I could jump free from blame. It didn't for some reason, momentary fatigue or the like, decidedly not from self-discipline.

With a heavy sigh, sort of reciprocating, I added:

"You can't expect somebody, say, a smoker, to quit an ingrained bad habit until the right moment, the moment he is ready."

"Who is the smoker, if I may ask?"

"One of us. In fact, Carlos is a smoker now."

"Yes, I know, and don't dodge the question."

"Both of us, then, as you wish."

I was dissatisfied with myself. To be witty, I had unintentionally taken on half of the blame, a pity, as I would have liked to include an innuendo about which of us kicked up this fuss.

"You don't exactly have to throw flowers at his feet, you know. And if he was so harsh, I'm sure it wasn't from spite," she added, as if knowing my thoughts.

*

Like a raptor striking its prey, a new thought hit me. It may not have been so much from stress or spite as from pride or conceit? With his MBA, he expected money from my tree of prosperity; it needed just a little shaking, or less, as he was entitled to it. And there I was with a denigrating cliché about giving them a hand, like being ready to help clean out the attic or something.

Yes, this thought stands to reason – so, too, does another guess; that I had got a good look at an embarrassing situation, which was a direct consequence of their Noble Knight ideas on thermometers, blood tests and what-not; had cleared it up, too, and that in front of Elif, all of which was trenching on the respect due to him. Pride and conceit again, was it?

22

"We are in the process of upgrading our business activities," he said.

I had met Carlos only a few times since our showdown, and he had not been disposed to talk about his work. Until now.

He had invited us for a late lunch at one of the small beachside eating places, *Hotty Café*. Like the other single-storied wooden structures there, it had its gable turned towards the beach, but in contrast to most of them, it was still open – and therefore also well frequented, particularly by Turks and half-stationary expats. Who was staff and who was guest was difficult to tell at first. Most of the customers behaved in a familiar way, talking across tables and exchanging dishes with each other.

We had had no feeling that something was in the wind.

"Oh," I said, "is that so?"

"Yes, time for a great leap forward now."

As *Great Leap Forward* had been Mao Zedong's dictum, I reflected, Carlos' choice of words may have been coincidental. Or else it was modern business jargon turning Mao upside down. Anyway, my memory told me the Great Helmsman had led his people to destruction, although my pinkish student generation had been keen on denying it at the time.

"Yes, we are taking down our shingle here," he said, and nodded three or four times in the way many do nowadays (rather few Turks, though), "and moving to Italy. It's going to be a truly high-profile venture. At sea." And with a mild giggle, he added: "We will rule the waves."

"It's going to be on a boat?"

"On board ship, yes."

Instead of making gestures in the air, as maybe many of his contemporaries would have done, he was sitting with arms crossed over his chest, a favourite position in certain situations. No mistaking his contentment.

"Not just any ship, I can tell you. I should say she is something between *Regal Princess* and *Crystal Symphony*, quite big. Haven't seen her yet myself."

After a few moments, while Madeleine and I were busy reining in our gasping astonishment, he continued:

"We have a rental contract – but may end up buying it. Both options are on the table."

I don't know much about big ships, although my high school teacher, a calendar freak, told us the length of the *Titanic*: 260 metres something. Was Carlos' ship more or less that? Something held me from asking. True, I rather wanted to know the price tag, which paradoxically made me even less inclined to enquire about it.

Yet, for his sake, I would be glad, of course; he had run out of breath, one could understand, and now there was a second wind.

We were seated next to the entrance, if that's the right word for an open gable. Some palms and a clump of Indian pearl trees, the seeds of which in earlier days were used for Turkish prayer beads, stood glittering on the other side of the dirt road and framed the sea view for us. Every few minutes, a young woman in a miniskirt passed our table with dishes in her hands, then tripping along on a green artificial grass rug across the road (green at least when rolled out in the morning) and on into the grove, giving the impression that the latter was but a natural outgrowth of the restaurant – very likely in contravention of the Regulation of Streets and Buildings Act, if there is one – and returning light on her feet with a trail of merry laughter behind her.

There was also a lady of about twice her age, far more modestly dressed, doing the same tour, though with less speed and enough time to make comments and nod at us: "Our library is for you!"

Out of courtesy, I turned towards the metre-high bookcase behind me filled with well-thumbed books. Perhaps left behind by guests, I thought, and started to look at the stack on top: *Phototherapy for Inner Growth;* under this, a heavily used *Alternate Nostril Breathing;* under this again, a book by a Dr Marella on anxiety and stress safely resting on *Alternatives Leben: Ein Handbuch*, as thick as all the others put together. Are Germans any good at alternative living? I wondered.

Intuitively, I now knew who the owner of Hotty Café was: an oldish man who was walking barefoot between the tables without looking really busy with anything, in fact, looking quite alternative himself: peculiar trousers, long hair and beard. No way to tell whether he wore a pendant, too.

Carlos drained his beer at a draught – more than one; it must have been, as it was a huge glass – and then the older woman, forty-something, slim like a tulip stem and speaking with an accent, which may have been Dutch, hastened to bring him another without him even ordering it. Certainly, if he used to express displeasure with most things, Turkish EFES beer was a glaring exception, and, quite likely, if my stomach stood alcohol, I might well have been an EFES aficionado myself.

With affected or genuine casualness, Carlos was sitting with one arm flung over the back of his chair, explaining that they planned to launch an international *epistemic* corporation, or possibly a foundation – still to be registered, hence no official name yet; it was a three-legged *forum-function*, or maybe he said *forum-enhancing* enterprise, for internationally high-profile people. And, needless to say, with cash flows accordingly.

Impossible to remember his exact words, of course, but something along those lines. I remember the word *epistemic* clearly, because I didn't know it, couldn't even be sure it was an economic term.

Madeleine, nicely tanned, wearing her Swedish summer dress with printed meadow flowers in honour of the day, looked as benevolent as she was tied up in knots, and asked Carlos about 'three-legged'.

"What does it mean?"

He took to using his hands. "Look, I would say we are experiencing a world of flux with serious challenges –economic crises, wars, terrorism, what have you. More than serious: vital. The thrust of our work will be to bring three *epistemic* communities together. More concretely: international top people in business, politics and academe. Always balancing outstanding theory with practical accomplishments! This is our *signum* so to speak." He was nodding too.

I couldn't figure out why he was telling us all this; that is, for what purpose had he arranged this event? Just to say goodbye? Or to show that everything had gone his way? Grandstanding fashion. In any case, I couldn't free myself from the suspicion that he was also putting me to the test somehow. Let's take a flyer, I thought, so help me, *Financial Times*:

"Have you done a risk analysis?"

Of course, I didn't really know what a risk analysis meant unless it was about drawing a card from a deck – one chance in four to draw a spade, one in thirteen to pick a jack. (Or maybe fourteen?) Anyway, my newspaper had taught me that for a business undertaking to be successful, you should consider the chance that things may turn out differently from what you plan.

"Risk analysis? Look, my partner's father is an Egyptian lawyer, financial counsel, linked to a shipping company, who will take care of things like that."

He may have taken my question as a sign of interest, or otherwise. I couldn't tell which. In any case, his referral to an Egyptian lawyer wasn't really what I expected to hear.

"Fine, good," I said.

Young people might be inclined to brush off risks as nothing but small irritants, buzzing gnats, whereas older people might perceive them as predators ready to slice you to pieces. What would this Egyptian be inclined to see? Nile mosquitoes or Nile crocodiles?

Though sitting self-absorbed, I could hear Madeleine and Carlos had started chatting about Sicily, where they were to be based; about this island as a showcase of beautiful ceramics. A pottery enthusiast, Madeleine wanted to tell him about Sicily's capital of porcelain, a bit north of Syracuse, called the Castle of Jars by the Arabs in the distant past. "And there is this monumental majolica staircase, Carlos! We could meet up there sometime, the three of us," she said, and looked at me in a happy, persuasive way. "In the summer, when it's decorated with lovely flowers all the way to the top!"

"Yea," I said lamely, "why not."

Almost physically, I could feel my shrinking desire to partake in even this kind of harmless conversation. I needed to reason with myself, excusing myself if you like.

It's far too late now to be constructive, if that's what I want. Anyhow, Carlos only wants comments that can be accommodated in the castle of thought he has built for himself, those which only scratch the surface and don't move a load-bearing wall or something, much less aim to tear down the whole shebang –

which is rather natural, in a way, I have to admit.

Our coffee was served by the young girl. It was like her black denim skirt was even shorter when she came closer to us, certainly when she bent forward, and besides, it was kept together by a studded seam that didn't close tightly, and probably wasn't meant to.

Madeleine wrinkled her nose at either or both defects, no telling which, whereas Carlos fiddled with his glasses and began poking among the books in the bookcase. I myself was all at sea, as if no longer familiar with natural behaviour. Looking the other way is an art, too.

The owner came with a cake. Yes, his hair was very bushy, his beard also, one passing seamlessly into the other.

A three-layer sponge cake "On the House!," he said as he put this impressive pastry in the middle of the table with a big shining grin that made me instantly revise his age down twenty years or so. His long, dark canvas shorts had slits on either leg, but strangely placed, so they could hardly be pockets. I got a feeling he was the spider in the air I had seen some days earlier from our house.

On leaving us, he waved at Carlos in a high-five sort of way, and why not, as Carlos was the one footing the bill, but this got me wondering whether they might be friends. I could have asked Carlos about that but chose a different question:

"Do you go paragliding?"

"Yes."

Somehow I didn't expect this answer. "How do you steer?"

"There are handles."

"And strings to pull, perhaps?"

"That too."

"Pretty much like running a business," I suggested, with a gleam in my eye, which should have been more eye-catching perhaps.

Carlos sat silent for a moment.

"You're telling me."

At this farewell meal, he had had his eyes turned alternately towards Madeleine and me, but no more so than they wandered about every now and then –like a recalcitrant politician who has had a press conference forced on him. Could be he didn't give a damn, at least not about me. A perfunctory lunch more than anything else, a piece of roguery.

Well, it happens in the best families, it would appear, and so we must make do with what we have and make the best of it; and many of us shouldn't ask for more when it comes to the crunch.

I know myself to be a bad diplomat. My mission was difficult, though; Carlos wants us to share his joy, which is all right so far as it goes, but there is a thin line between joy and conceit, however skilfully cloaked, and I see him as on the wrong side.

*

On arrival in Turkey, Carlos must have looked up to me as an admirable success. Since then, the telescope has turned around: he sees a skinflint curmudgeon who has tried to pull the wool over his eyes. And I must admit the fault is all mine, as my strategy of choice, if strategy it was, was always to tiptoe.

23

Madeleine felt too tired to drive herself all the way to Kemer, so we set out for a walk to the taxi stand at the entrance of Liman. As coincidence would have it, we passed by the 'alternative' eating place we visited with Carlos only a week before. The owner ran out to meet us and showered us with a profuse welcome. He was barefoot; such soles are not for ordinary people.

Still patting my back, he started to talk about Carlos. With large mandibular movements, he praised his paragliding; whether Carlos had been his pupil or his instructor we didn't understand, but evidently Carlos had, more than once, sailed out into the bay all the way to the 'black tooth', behind which the bay ends and the open sea begins.

He somehow got us inside and seated us at the same table as last time, rather as if we were regulars now.

"Your son is as skilful a businessman as he is a paraglider," he declared.

And then, taking with him a stunning woman, he continued, giving two quick winks, which from a hairy face like his makes quite an impact.

With a series of diffuse gestures, Madeleine silent as if drifting in abstraction, I indicate that all that was completely beyond me. Carlos was *Born on the Night of Destiny*, he said at last. Although we didn't quite follow – born with the caul, like Napoleon, was it? – neither of us cared to ask. This was beginning to be too much of a good thing. Yes, overkill.

Eating Turkish *lahmacun* pizza, known as sex on the beach (ingredients no more salacious than prawn, anchovy and tomatoes), we gave way to guessing about the possible nature of the friendship between Carlos and the owner. It struck us that everything about Carlos seemed to move quickly, and we were obviously not the first stop.

I fell on my *Financial Times*, eagerly as if it were a fresh newspaper, although in fact it always reaches me one or even two days late. Well, who cares, when you are in the middle of nowhere, where news seldom if ever has direct implications? There were several reports on the EU's *travails* – well, well, well. A short article on Turkey: the PKK has let loose a new offensive, which I already knew. A small, outlying place like this is definitely out of range.

Imagine my surprise when Madeleine pulled *How to Spend It* from her brown travel bag, as I know this magazine riles her, littered with fashion as it always is. Only hours earlier had I thrown this particular issue straight into the bin in the laundry room – true to my habit; FT supplements to do with fashion, jewellery, collecting and the like always face this certain doom.

The bar was half-full of locals and she seemingly wanted no one to monitor her reading; she held her hands in an odd, protective way, like a poker player; only her cards were too large to be protected efficiently. However, if she was obscuring her activities, or at least trying to, she could by no means hide her reactions.

She was flipping through pages, back and forth between black and white photos taken in car scrapyards, with model after model perched on junked cars, each vehicle in a worse condition than the last, it appeared, as if brought in from some car-torching ritual in suburban Paris or somewhere.

"Alas, this suffering woman!"

She pointed with her right-hand index finger – her fingers strong with short-cut nails, although otherwise she was rather fine-boned – but didn't care much to show me the picture, which I got to view upside down.

"Look, so sad in spite of her 18 ct gold and oxidised-silver necklace!"

"Ungrateful," I suggested.

Although I couldn't read her countenance from my perspective, I could tell her legs were uncommonly wide apart, 3.5 on a scale of 5, while she was sitting on the front of a, to all appearances, filthy scrap vehicle, left arm supported by her long thighs, hand over crotch.

"Rings in gold and silver with white and black diamonds from £1000," supplied Madeleine in a contentedly patronising tone.

"Not everything is money, you know," I said cheerfully.

She gave me a quick glance. Reproachfully, or so I thought, although there was no counterpoint to be seen, such as a squinting or furrowed brow.

While we're on the subject, when we first met, Madeleine had no facial wrinkles at all, but twenty years leave traces of course. At a guess, it was first that her cheeks had come down a little.

I was in for another surprise when she again flipped up her round travel bag, which, always leaning wearily (as the leather was cut by unskilled hands), stood at her feet, and produced a second issue of *How to Spend It* that I couldn't even remember having seen, although I took its origin to be from the same waste container.

"Well now," I said. Just that, nothing more.

"I tell you, I read it sometimes, but I have to sift what I see, sifting it through my eyelashes."

I looked at those. Above her ordinary nose a pair of blue-green eyes, not very deep-set, rather the contrary, like the old portraits of Swedish princesses, but her thinning lashes could not possibly be up to the task.

She lingered at a page adorned with a half-length portrait of a woman in a verdant dress with flourishing vegetation in the background – the woman herself in her *Green Salad Days*, I thought smugly, nice to be able to use a little Shakespeare every now and then – a young creature, very much so, with low hairline and mouth half-open.

"Now, from here, this model doesn't seem to be of the cut-glass type, or is she?"

"No, she's an exception. But there is too much of it," meaning too stylish, I supposed. She was a model for Graff, the jewellery company, and was generously strewn with precious stones.

"Don't look at the prices," I suggested.

At that, Madeleine smiled; and yes, I remember, I made some kind of additional observation for my hypothesis on facial counterpoint: her fine crow's feet were indeed set in motion. Not much to build a theory on, I admit.

Just as Madeleine was about to put the magazine away, I noted a dark dot sitting on the shoulder of the diamonds beauty – a real beauty she most likely was – a little away from the neckline to one side, and, bang, my stiff index finger was out to point it out.

"Could be a *mouche* or a birthmark, my best guess, but I…"

"That has nothing to do with it!" Madeleine snapped.

Only seldom does she approve of my dermatological excesses, and never when she has other fish to fry.

"Do we have to receive these ludicrous supplements? Tell them we want to be relieved of them."

"All of them?"

"Yes, *Silly Mode* and *Unnecessary Gems* and *Fat Motorcycles*, what have you. That smaller one too – *Wealth,* is it? You don't read it, do you?"

"I doubt it can be done," I tried, silently giving praise for her naming mockery.

"Write to them. It's a terrible waste of paper."

"No go, I can't do it. Digital news is knocking paper news out of business these days – and here comes somebody asking one of the losers for special treatment. A Turk to boot."

"Turk? No one can tell from your name; and, besides, you have dual nationality."

I shook my head but didn't want to seem unreasonable, and thought a little sliver of humble pie wouldn't be out of place.

"I'm with you if you write a letter."

"You are the subscriber, not me," she replied in a prickly fashion.

Unlike us, I thought, to wrangle about such a trifling matter, even if only petite-wrangling it was.

24

As we are leaving Hotty Café, the owner comes over with the cologne bottle and, naturalised Turk as I am, I like the ceremony and don't even mind letting it be a lengthy one. He is a peculiar man but a likable personality. A bit religious in one way or another, but whether a true Muslim seems doubtful.

So while Madeleine was heading for the taxi stand, I stood postprandial, chatting a little with him (again, forgive my medical jargon) about his idea to reserve part of the shore as a nesting beach for sea turtles, if I remember correctly, before I made for the grocery store to pick up some supplies with my now sweet-smelling hands.

I chanced on an old friend. On a narrow strip of common land, some dogs were lying together under a canopy under which, in high season, some ladies from the village used to sit in their *salwar* trousers, baking flatbread on a big domed griddle, Turkish folk music streaming out from a ghetto blaster behind: *When I went to Skutari I found a handkerchief...*

The light-coloured creature in the middle... could it possibly be the puppy that had caught me flat-footed when I was googling Carlos? Well, not really unawares, but I had had shut down my search, hadn't I?

Curious to know, I stopped and took a good long look, trying to stare her up from her resting place. Unexpectedly, I must say, she did rise after a while, as if to take the measure of me, and started to walk towards me without making any hurry about it, until she came quite close.

No question about it, it was her. Not a puppy any longer; otherwise, the same; those velvet-ears and almond-eyes with black lines above and below them. When I bent down and cupped my hands around her soft, warm skull, she eagerly reached to give me a lick on my mouth. Better not, I thought, and took my leave without saying goodbye, to be on the safe side so to speak.

It didn't take long to gather together the articles I wanted, as I know my way around in Kerim's crammed shop, which he has named Paradise. Madeleine and I called it Purgatory; windows only around the entrance and anaemic lamps in the roof (almost none in the back), which make Kerim, who has a criss-cross of lines on his face and a little sorrowful mouth, look far sterner than he otherwise would.

I picked butter and a yoghurt drink from the refrigerated cabinet halfway into the darkness; eggplants (in Turkish, *shakshuka*, a delicacy), celeriac and carrots a few shelves further away; chocolate closer to the exit (and, alas, closer to the warm); wine and mineral water nearby (tourist articles, pride of place) –then it came to a halt. What else did I want? I couldn't concentrate, because of the elephant in my mind, that dog.

Kerim came up to me with a pack of silicone heel wedges he had ordered for me quite some time ago and which I had nearly forgotten all about. It was on account of my idea of breaking my record for reaching the summit of the west mountain, where the wireless communication tower is. Forty-five minutes: I could do better. Stupid perhaps, considering my age.

"Autumn is approaching," I said.

"Huh? Yes, on its way."

"Winter here is neither cold nor very long. But rainy and desolate. Can be hard on the dogs, the homeless ones."

Strange in a way, I had never spared their autumnal predicament a thought before. Yet three autumns had already passed.

"So what will happen to them, do you think?"

Kerim shrugged in his black vest, his preferred shop coat (in contrast to his wife, always in white) and started weighing my carrots. After some moments, he gave a reply:

"Those in... *bad shape*... will be taken for a ride in the mountains, I presume."

"A ride in the mountains?" I repeated, standing like a fool on the other side of the weighing scale. "Who does that?"

"I'm not involved," he said.

"Ah, who is?"

"Go and ask Orhan Bey."

"Orhan Bey," I repeated, like he was unknown to me, which he wasn't, far from it.

"Yes, the grocer down the other end."

"Ah, him."

The location of the store is better and there is a terrace facing the street, but it still has fewer customers. Outside, an official green Jeep was parked. A *gendarme* was sitting in one of the plastic chairs, which had once probably been yellow, with his cap on the table in front of him, ice cream cone in one hand, the other flicking through newspapers with big headlines: *Police Bus Attacked in Diarbakir*.

I could see Orhan Bey standing in front of the cash register with an unusual expression. Normally, he is smiling all the time, like an American presidential candidate, which is far from normal Turkish behaviour, if you ask me. Just now, he has his shoulders raised, heron style.

In front of him, behind the counter, there was a man who could be an inspector or something, perhaps controlling his licence or cash register. This certainly dissuaded me from crossing the threshold, yet so much more pleasurable would it be to shout inside:

Mr Inspector, that guy charged me for two Hürriyet, chancing I was stupid enough to believe the local pages were a separate newspaper – my three lira, are they still there in his secret drawer?

Needless to say, it wasn't the money, but his impudence.

A few minutes, I lingered on the terrace. This was a quiet afternoon and I could only hear the crickets and a lorry some way off, presumably the water delivery truck. The young *gendarma* looked up, his face all in a sweat and ice cream at the corners of his pouting mouth, twenty-five at the very most.

"Not all newspapers care to brand the PKK as terrorists any longer," he muttered. "They call them Kurdish Patriots, ha!"

Since this was said in Turkish, he probably knew me, by name if nothing else, and why not, as the foreign colony isn't big, could be two dozen, and the two of us are the only ones with Turkish citizenship, and besides, never mix with the others. I confined myself to vaguely – or rather lugubriously – nodding in agreement.

So as not to strike up a real conversation, I lost no time in going back into the shop. To buy cucumbers, I decided. They go well with fried celeriac slices, which is another favourite dish. Also, as I had heard from Fatosh, many dogs like cucumber a lot.

25

Madeleine entertained a correspondence of sorts with Carlos. For every two or three of her neatly handwritten letters, she got a reply by mail. It's quite possible of course that for him, handwriting was a long-since-passed stage of personal development.

There wasn't much to extract about his doings, and a prickly feeling sometimes popped up inside me, not Madeleine, that this wasn't just his regular buttoned-up-ness. Was this his way of rapping me over my knuckles?

Quite unexpectedly, the *Financial Times* came to our assistance.

Zia handed me a substantial wad of well-fed newspapers in a big shopping plastic bag. It said *Antalya Elektronik* on it; perhaps he had taken the plunge at last and bought this MacBook Air, for which he had no real use (twelve hours' battery time, one charge lasting several months for him).

"Heavy, these pink things," he said, grinning.

"You know why? Cos they come with much fatter headlines these days – *Global Warming, Arms Race, Economic Downturn…* burdensome things," I said, hoping as usual he hadn't taken a peep into some supplement unsuitable for him, such as *Watches* or *Wealth*.

We start vilifying the weather, no difficult task.

It was autumnal now; the sky one day flooded with sunlight, next couple of days flooded with fine drops of water coming so tightly that the top of the cliff in the middle of the bay could not be seen; otherwise, the only thing pertaining to the sea visible from our upstairs windows. Unimpaired sunny days were rare now; small birds were fewer and further between, and telephone wires looked miserably naked. Along one of the smaller roads leading up to the main costal road, at the Petrol Ofisi and the village sewage plant, embankments were being undermined.

We had to step aside for people in overalls who passed through the lobby with hoses and machines.

"Is your basement leaking?" Madeleine asked.

"Yes, for the first time in my years here. Not serious, though. On the other hand, we have wild fires, so it isn't as though we get less than we should," he replied with a chuckle.

"This side in particular," he said, pointing with a hand that had certainly been in the garden soil that day through the little window, which is too high up to peer out at anything but the sky.

"The fire once crept so close that the wall was singed. Never this time of the year, though," he said, grinning once more.

One of the nicest things about him is his sense of humour.

*

Protected from inundation as our own house was, thanks to it lacking a cellar, it was not immune from trouble with the electricity. No sooner had we sat down in the living room easy chairs, to satisfy our hunger for news from the plastic bag, than the lamp bulbs started to flicker irritatingly.

This happens every now and then; could be something to do with the grid, or, these days, humidity in the transformer shed. Who are we to know? Yet we don't like the idea of a noisy reserve generator in the scullery; why forego our peace and quiet? We chose this place partly because of its peacefulness.

So we made haste through the drizzle to Hotty Café, which, in contrast to most other eateries, doesn't close down in autumn and is open on weekdays. In fact, it has become our regular spot.

The open gable was now covered by a vinyl curtain with a flap door. Inside, there was heat like the height of summer as the pizza oven had been on for a couple of hours. On and off, the vinyl wall shuddered and the horizontal planks of the wall creaked, gusts coming down from the Taurus. Walking across the grove outside, down to the beach, you could see a mountaintop which was snow-capped half of the year and about to be so now.

"Can we have two *Sex on the Beach* in an hour," I asked the Dutchwoman, whom we now knew to be half-German and a psychotherapist (with a certificate from some faraway place). We assume she is the partner of the owner, and him we have baptised Mr Hotty.

I set out to wade through the newspapers before tucking into the sinful pizza. Ten minutes per issue, at the very most, they hardly matter more.

It's good to get them belatedly; big news becomes smaller by itself. I have a feeling I have said it before; yea, a bit of a barrel organ sometimes.

Madeleine was leafing through a Saturday/Sunday issue at random.

"*Basel two*, what's that? Isn't Basel just Basel?"

I dipped into my shallow well of knowledge: something about regulation, no doubt, about banks, could be. After these few words, she had had enough of it but came up with a new question after a couple of minutes with the weekend supplement *Life and Art*, which presumably resonated better with her interests.

"What's *Power Dressing?*"

"What?"

"There is an article about it."

Arms resting on the table, she reads aloud to me in a remarkably satisfied tone: the Prime Minister gave a speech in which the brands he was wearing were listed. Shirt from… somewhere… underpants from Marks & Spencer. "Interesting, really, don't you think?" she ended.

This was subtle humour in my style, just that the humour part of it was minor.

"Well, that says it all, doesn't it?"

"Not quite, Birger. There is also this fifty-six-year-old man, president of something, who says: 'Whenever I'm out, I always buy handkerchiefs. I probably have over fifty now.'"

She stares at me. Promptingly.

"You don't have any power handkerchiefs, do you?"

"Oh, I'm not completely without, the one bought at the market after I had been picking my cuticles, remember? Blue flower on it, embroidered. Stands out nicely against the blood patch.

"Still going strong, it is," I added.

"What is?"

"The blood spot."

"I'm glad to know you do not belong in that category," she concluded, a broad smile to match.

"Oh no, not me. Put me into the *Gilded Misfit Dressing*," I said happily, and pinched my dirt-yellow corduroy trousers – of which half the ribs, or whatever the stripes are called – had become mercilessly de-corded by the ravages of time.

"Also known as *Retrograde Ego Style*," I added. "At conferences, I was always the only one sporting *Id Minus Apparel*."

"What do you mean by Id?"

"Yourself, according to Freud et al."

Now she seemed to be incontrovertibly happy.

The plastic door was pushed aside and in strode Mr Hotty with an impressive pile of cardboard boxes for the kitchen, a mound of tomatoes in the top one. We could see little more of him than two hairy lower legs –my anatomy teacher called them *crus*, Latin of course, never heard it since – and his feet. For an *alternative man,* there were unusually well-pedicured feet in the flip-flop sandals, at any rate compared with mine, mismanaged if you ask Madeleine. He has age on his side.

Behind him, a guest sneaked in, an elderly man, somewhat bent with white hair and a dark complexion, and immediately settled in his favourite corner, where he put a well-used booklet on the table together with a brown rosary. People in Turkey are known to look Oriental or Nordic or anything in between, but in my eyes, his colour wasn't natural; pathologic rather, a VSOP face.

A *Zoroastrian,* Hotty told us. As there are so many varieties of Islam, I took it to be some kind of outlying Muslim sect.

"Oh no, our friend's religion is Living Peacefully, also to live praying. Whereas Muslims pray five times a day, these pray many more times. Can you imagine?"

I didn't feel inclined to delve deeper into the topic. Yet, despite being a non-believer and praying zero times a day, I somehow sympathised with him; who isn't for living peacefully?

I was not wont to read the short news items in the economy section of the newspaper – the longer ones suited my learning aims better. This time, however, by pure coincidence, I did. Or was it that my peripheral vision had perceived the caption and I had unconsciously allowed myself to be captured by a keyword?

> *The successful* International Paladine, *registered in Sicily and providing executive coaching programmes for businesses on three continents, is currently negotiating*

with the well-known Egyptian shipbroker firm Gross & Sayedi, *which has made a bid for the purchase of* International Paladine's *cruise ship* Roger II.

The luxury vessel is fully equipped for international meetings, conferences and workshops at sea, including a helipad, gym and running track.

Agreeing the contract under negotiation, the seller would unlock resources of upwards of US$100 million for a yet more dynamic expansion of Paladine, geographically as well as substantially, and lease back the vessel from Gross & Sayedi. Dr Sayedi is the father of one of the three owners of the seller company.

Ah!

I shook my head in disbelief – then gave a handful of extra shakes, as it is always good if you have loose crystals in your inner ear – and reread it more carefully, not without a queer feeling in my stomach.

Carlos has bowled me over, I admit that, I kept saying to myself. Just accept it.

With my blue felt tip that is always in the trouser pocket, I started drawing a circle around the notice, which had a strong decorative impact against the salmon newsprint. I held up the page in front of Madeleine, who at first didn't look where she was supposed to, but finally started reading it, perhaps rereading too, as it took some time.

"Fantastic!" she cried. And then in a second: "Good news, isn't it?" Her eyes were wide open.

"No doubt about it. He has got a fair wind," I said.

Normally, Madeleine never takes on a breathless look, other than when she is on to a bird she has never seen before, a real rarity like a *roseatae spoonbill* or something. This one was no doubt very exotic.

I said, "I am so glad for your sake, Madeleine, and his sake." Usually we have no reason to use each other's first name.

And then, it seemed to me, I should say: "For my part, of course, it's a walk to Canossa." When Madeleine didn't understand, I added: "Like this pig-headed German emperor had to do. On his knees."

"No, Birger. Nothing of the kind. But why don't you send him a letter? I'm sure he would appreciate it."

As if to underscore my fresh humility, I darted across the room – there were very few guests – and into the kitchen with my paper, which I left spread out on the tomatoes on top of the box pile that had just been brought in. Mr Hotty, a skinned flatfish in his hand, gave it a perplexed glance and I asked the Dutchwoman to translate it for him.

There was a big commotion in the kitchen.

Within minutes, they were standing at our table sparkling with pleasure and best wishes, Mr Hotty swinging a bottle of *raki* and a little Turkish ice-cream flag. He gave a thumbs-up with one hand and held a flag up with the other while the Dutchwoman filled our glasses.

"Hats off to Carlos," I exclaimed, and Mr Hotty began a solemn announcement:

"As a chef…" he began, and continued with something we failed to understand until his helper supplied it in English:

"Being a chef, I know Carlos is well worth his salt."

*

As I said, I was glad for Madeleine – for Carlos too, though only up to a point. To tell the truth, I wasn't quite at ease.

Dignity galled? Yes, I plead guilty, but there was also my

wondering – or possibly my dignity once again, although cloaked – about whether the article said it all. I couldn't help turning a sneaking suspicion over in my mind. A first-class idea, be it about politics, business or whatever, may turn out well but can be ill-fated too, of course. Just as a bad idea may turn out bad – or, however unexpectedly, bring luck. However, how is it that they can set free one hundred million dollars in capital that they had borrowed?

Careful now! These thoughts could set me on a slippery slope. Stop it before it's too late.

*

There's a poem pinned on the board by my computer, written by hand on the back of a sheet from some promotional notepad or other. I don't remember when or why I wrote it, in a moment of particular inspiration. As with many other things on the board, the yellow fangs of time have been chewing on this slip, leaving it brittle and rough.

> 'His helm was sensitivity.
> His star was that of fantasy.
> Heading toward seventy:
> Islet of Maturity!'

It's short with fine rhymes. On these merits it can stay there, but the exclamation mark jars with me.

26

On the beach just behind the grove in front of the Hotty Café, Zia's brother had rigged a large market tent. There was a pleasant smell of soil, tomatoes and asparagus about, and no wonder, as he was a greengrocer.

Already before it was completely raised, musicians had begun to play in front of it, *dombek* drums and elegiac flutes, even a long neck lute, and many men were dancing with raised hands. A bonfire was lit with split wood from the back of a Ford Transit (made in Turkey) parked at the tent side, which added considerably to the spirit of the event.

This was the Thursday afternoon; the party itself was starting the following afternoon.

Having a big sixtieth birthday feast did not chime with Zia's preferences: he couldn't see the point in it, but in the end he bowed to his big brother, Abi Bülent, who was a recognised party animal, as fond of the Turkish kitchen as of its *raki*, and who triumphantly wore his waist measurement, according to Zia, his own unchanged since adolescence.

Holy Mother of God, I had a tremendous party, Zia, so no less for you! Well heeled and generous too, Bülent Bey offered to take care of it all, which certainly shook up Zia's hierarchy of preferences. The terms of surrender were simple: fifty guests at the very most. But big brother used one of his most capacious tents – no others free, you see – which seats twice as many, and yet it was still crowded.

Almost immediately the food came, large trays of *mezeler* carried out, homemade, only to be expected, and leading to lively guesses about which households had made what. The party spirit was no less quick, all gaiety and toasts, and increasing as the evening progressed.

There were speeches, of course, with much praise: a fine paterfamilias, hard-working, reliable, helpful. A bit cut and dried, perhaps, but we also learned some other things; that he had been in the forces that Turkey landed on Cyprus in 1974 to protect the Turkish population there after the Greek colonels' coup. And that he was a tank-truck driver during the Gulf War, crossing the eastern border with Iraqi oil twice a week, which we had in fact heard before – and that he had carried other goods on board too. No one would guess what these were, at least not out loud.

We were sitting at narrow tables flanked by long benches, Madeleine and I somewhere in the middle, where we didn't know many faces, but most of them seemed to be dressed-up cousins and seemingly much younger than the 'birthday boy' himself.

When whole roast lambs were carried in by a troop of guests headed by Mr Hotty, there was a sudden hustle and bustle around Bülent, who seemed to stage some complicated, at any rate extended, castling at the honorary table. Leaving a substantial gap behind him, Bülent came to pick us up to take us to his side and thus closer to Zia, who sat there looking formal but contented in his dark suit and spotted silk tie. Zia's wife, Emel, in her late forties, looked equally content, as in fact she always does, a friendly red mouth nicely set between dimpled cheeks.

Bülent introduced us to some of the others, including the greenhouse leaser, Volkan, with whom I was already well acquainted, and who now used the opportunity to thank me for my shaving tips.

This was the first time I had met his face clean-shaven, full of lines and colours, such as a painter of portraits might like to depict, and, in Madeleine's view, plainly kindred to Zia's countenance. Chin uplifted, Volkan said: "In fact, my whole family is grateful for it!"

And Bülent quickly pulled a witticism with a big grin: "*Güneş balçıkla sıvanmaz*": you can't plaster over the sun with mud. Fond of Turkish proverbs as I am, even when I don't get their logic, I grinned back at him.

"Zia always was a motor freak," said Bülent. "His dream is to own a Lotus Evora. Fiery red! That boy over there – his eldest son, married, by the way, for many years now – same dream." That they were of similar height and build we could easily determine for ourselves. "And you have seen the girls, right? They take care of the waiting, together with the ladies."

They had a neat appearance, short-sleeved summer dresses. It was difficult to tell the difference in age; perhaps the plumpish girl was the younger.

"Elif?" Bülent said, and perhaps I could read a bit of surprise in his voice. "No, she isn't here," but he didn't expand, as his mind now seemed concentrated on something he was about to jot down on a scrap of paper already full of scribbles.

Presently, he rose from the table, and his eyes, a bit close-set, swept around the tent while his wife clinked her glass with a spoon for him. It's really something special to be sitting in the shadow of an imposing speaker.

"Dear friends! We all know Zia has many talents. Now I'm going to tell you more about one of them. Back when we were living with our parents, Zia wanted us to construct… a *motorcycle*. Quite something, right?"

Most of the chewing came to a halt as the audience stilled, savouring their expectations.

"Its name was to be *Büliza*, which in Ottoman days was the

name of the immortal *Golden Eagle* of the Toros Mountains."

No mistake, in front of his kin, he wasn't big brother Bülent, but rather Bülent the comedian.

"We strolled around the junk yards of Kayseri looking for motorcycle parts, an engine too, to piece together, and a welding torch. Everything was given to us free. They were kind to small boys, but I remember they warned us about the welding. Remember our farm in Kayseri? The barn furthest away from the house – that's where we went to work. Clear as day, we couldn't tell anyone what we were up to."

He paused and raised his glass – a liquid as clear as water. Cheers! If it was *raki*, there certainly wasn't any water in it.

"I was about fifteen, so you can work out for yourselves how old Zia was. He did the welding, as I am a little on the cautious side. Zia was never afraid of anything.

"We started from the principle: the more welds the better. How does that sound to you? Remember, we were self-taught."

Mrs Emel still wore her contented aspect, contented plus now. Zia was glowing.

"Which of you agree: the more welds, the better the end result?"

Laughs and movement; one after another, hands flew in the air.

"Well then, which of you think the opposite, less strong?"

There was a show of hands across the length and breadth of the tent, lots of laughter, and Bülent proposed a toast – one for *Zia*, another for *the Eagerness of Youth*.

"We pulled *Büliza* up to the top of a hill to get some assistance from gravity – the kick-start broke, you see. And it started immediately. Fantastic! Zia flung himself gallantly on, and me behind him – gallantly too, I suppose, even if it swayed a little.

"A rather long motorcycle this was, as I said. Or did I? About a metre between Zia and me. The chain we had been given was a bit on the generous side, you see."

Bursts of laughter, with almost no pause between them now.

"One metre, Zia, what do you think?"

"Me?" He shook his head eagerly. "I don't remember anything of this," he succeeded in saying.

"Well, I think you remember… Anyway, the engine was loud, to say the least, and there was a billow of smoke, but it worked. But can you believe, quite unexpectedly…"

You could catch a glimpse of a new kind of smile here and there in the tent, perhaps with a touch of melancholy cum nostalgia or something of that nature. There may have been those, of course, who had already heard this story, many times even. After all, he was the family stand-up.

"…Yes, all of a sudden Zia was sort of closer to me than before, and at the same time higher, if you understand me! And then things began to come loose –and clunk down on the road. Even the engine. And the rest of it in a heap. And we were lying there too, kicking about.

"Cars passed us and honked. We got panicky! At the double, we shoved the whole shebang into a ditch at the side of the road and ran off like crazy across the fields. We were really good at it – running, I mean."

When his audience had laughed its fill, Bülent turned to his little brother:

"Zia, you are made of one single piece, solid and stable, despite having experienced a lot both here in Turkey and Iraq and Syria – and, yes, I forget, in that mine pit in Germany. But you never had to be welded together. Let's keep it that way, Zia!"

Cheering!

Bülent sat down but within seconds got up again. However trained an adjutant his wife was, she didn't get a chance to clink her glass.

"Zia was a skilled gymnast as a youngster. He could do a triple flip!"

"No, no, Bülent, that wasn't me. It was my teacher," Zia shouted.

"Aaah, never mind, don't be petty now. Zia did triple flips but never broke!"

After this intensive merriment, Zia had to take a deep breath and started to wipe his eyes with his napkin, Emel likewise, whose cheeks were wetter than his and had reddened to the colour of the wine glass in front of her.

Now questions began to hail upon him: *Zia, was it really true? Were you hurt? Did your father get to hear about it?* He gave only vague waves in response. In any event, there was every sign he was perfectly happy with Bülent's performance.

For the acme of the evening, the tables were rearranged and yesterday's musicians entered together with a young woman whom it took some time to identify. Evidently, she was Zia's youngest daughter, now as unlike her former waitress self as a sparkler is to the royal fireworks. Her face heavily maquillaged with fiery lip colour, she was wearing bright yellow harem trousers and a silvery halter, and had brass finger-cymbals on each hand.

Madeleine and I had never seen belly dancing before.

They started at a moderate tempo but an exciting and, to my ears, irregular rhythm, like a heart patient with sick sinus syndrome. Everything was moving; feet, legs, arms, fingers and the belly of course. Never thought a pelvis could be that acrobatic.

"Fantastic," Bülent burst out, turning towards Madeleine and me: "Watch now, this is a rare skill, honestly! Sideways is easier. Meryem is extremely good; you must have the *technique* and the *belly* too. Nobody but her in this village now. Elif, you know, had it," he rumbled on emphatically.

We stand up for a better view and many are clapping their hands. I clap myself, also to knock down my over-attentiveness to Bülent a little bit. The tent had been opened up at both ends for want of air – pitch dark outside, yet you could discern numerous faces there, lured by the suggestive rejoicing; few attractions can rival such music.

Holding one lira in his hand and polishing it with the edge of his jacket sleeve, Zia approaches Meryem and with a big smile, places it on her forehead.

"She can flip it with her belly too," trumpets Bülent.

The musicians increase the tempo, but the faster the flutes and the shining goblet drums play, the quicker are Meryem's movements, above all her belly, and the safer the coin seems to lie a finger's breadth below the hairline on her back-tilted face – rather like Elif's, I thought; ample lips; strong, well-shaped teeth.

27

Well established as Carlos was, Madeleine was keen to see him in his professional environment, and visit potteries at the same time, but probably didn't hang on to these hopes for long since he kept underscoring his workload whenever they communicated. After much self-scrutiny, I had made clear that I was willing to come with her, tread the majolica steps and see all the pottery beauty that there was on the island; willing too, or at least prepared, to swallow my self-inflicted humiliation and confess before Carlos that I had misjudged him and was sorry for that.

We decided to make plans; why not a trip over Christmas and New Year? Although we weren't there yet, some interesting places and bathing to look forward to. Madagascar? Cuba? Cape Verde?

We went for Iceland. True, not a very hot place, cool even in summer, but there are hot springs year around and exoticism in abundance. A further consideration, if irrelevant of course, was that Iceland, according to my *Pinko* (Madeleine's nickname), was unique in handling the international bank crisis; they let banks collapse and went after reckless bankers.

An extraordinary vacation it turned out to be.

Winter is perfect for walking inside glaciers, so we explored their surreal, blue beauty, and went on a whale-watching tour too, though without spotting real whales, but *killer whales*, voracious dolphins that feed on whales and other prey, including white sharks. Showing their black and white colouring, they came hunting in packs while a storm was blowing up. The little boat turned back, roller-coastering in the rough sea with only me on deck, on the bow; should have known better of course, thrillingly happy about my unexpected courage.

This happened in the first days, before we had by pure chance met the hotel doctor, Ingthor – Icelanders use their first names rather than surnames – with whom we shared a dinner table one evening. Tall and heavyset, he wore a hand-knitted wool sweater large enough to hold both me and Madeleine, and a bow tie with ducks on it. He told us he loved his country in all seasons but particularly in the winter when he used to go ptarmigan hunting. "Alas, last year I turned fifty and wanted to put myself to the test, and now as a doctor in the NATO mission, I am banished for three months to Kabul. So, if you want, you are welcome to use my lava field cabin! It is less than an hour's drive from a small town, westward, at Borgarfjordur Bay."

As we had landed at Keflavik Airport a couple of days earlier, I got a feeling this was going to be a *Premium Mind-Wash*, and taking up residence in this white lava field now confirmed it. Not least when, after a long walk, we were sitting in the hot tub, which we did at least twice a day, with our heads sticking out of the water between floating glasses and bowls, the snow falling; it seemed outright stupid, even preposterous, to think about things in our ordinary lives, and if someone had even asked me where Turkey was, it might have needed a little thought. A lovable estrangement and, not to be overlooked, a bonus for Madeleine's skin.

Unexpectedly, we had a couple of fine birding occurrences. On an excursion in the north, to broaden our horizons, we first drove to Akureyri, then on to Mývatn, a protected wetland known for its duck species (though without expecting much birdlife to speak of, the day before Christmas), where we took a dip in the Nature Bath, and next visited its restaurant; salmon soup with 'geyser bread', invigorating ourselves for a final visit to the Bird Museum.

That's where Madeleine spotted a small seabird with pink underparts that she had never seen before, and later identified as a Ross's gull, an arctic bird, all the more exciting as it shouldn't really be pink at this time of the year. A cool bird, pleasingly quiet if you ask me.

Down in Borganess, close to the bridge across the bay, where we had gone to resupply, we met another bird, far less exotic but still fascinating, in my view, to the degree that I wished the flying dreams I used to have –before my exhaustion had finally caught up with me –would return in rejuvenated form.

Sitting in the Geirabakari Coffee House, through its panoramic windows, we could observe a black sea bird in the air close to the bridge over the bay. The storm petrel, Madeleine explained – go and take a look!

And yes, I decided to stretch my legs and walk to the bridgehead. Almost no wind, not where I was standing. The bird above was perfectly still, inert like a watchful pike, not even a fin-stroke. I stood staring at it until I felt pain in my neck.

A frequent dream flyer, I had been sailing around notable buildings, such as Stockholm City Hall, touching the golden crowns on its spire, or the Karolinska Institute, where I worked as a junior doctor, or inside them, and over trees and gatherings, friends and foes –just a matter of fluttering fingers and toes, an occasional breast stroke perhaps, always surprised that I was the only one who knew the technique.

And now I really looked forward to taking my old dreams to a new level, floating up there above the bridgehead like this petrel, without even flapping for it.

PART III

28

The email had been as short as it was unexpected: *Will you be around next week? If so, I shall pop in.*

In other words, Madeleine's scion would substantiate himself after all these IRT months, if you will excuse me for this silly acronym, so easily mistaken for *Iesus Rex Temporalis* or something by all those living outside the world of email, Facebook, Twitter or whatever – the virtual-world expats.

Particularly for Madeleine, this was going to be a significant family event; Carlos had been in her thoughts a great deal, as he had in mine, although less so, presumably, and not necessarily for the same reasons.

I had just completed an inspection sweep of the house: the window frames needed painting and I would hire someone; the roof was in good enough shape after a carpenter-neighbour had helped with the ridge tiles; the sagging gutters I was still intent on tackling myself, the brackets patiently waiting in the garden shed, but as there was no real danger yet, I was instead dealing with the garden table.

Carlos found me behind the house where I was nailing new slats onto it. Sporting a baseball cap, three-quarter pants and sandals, he wasn't at all dressed as I expected, but certainly this gave him a new air and somehow even made him seem a bit slimmer, not that he was ever on the plump side, of course.

Or had it rather to do with his glasses?

"You no longer wear glasses?"

"I'll explain later," he replied, perhaps wanting to wait for Madeleine's return so as not to have to repeat himself.

Maybe a visit to an eye clinic to smooth his corneas, I thought.

Madeleine had gone for her second daily dip. In contrast to most tourists, she shies away neither from cold water nor, as now, from the turtle faeces bobbing in the water, and so may be the only one in the water right now. She is not the only one round here with eczema – I am often consulted by people about their skin, even trekkers pop in – but she is by far the most resolute.

Carlos took a nap on the sitting room sofa while I finished the nailing and, in haste, made an apple and almond cake, the only one I know how to bake, to be served with North Cypriot brandy.

Not until we were seated under the big cedar – which is good enough as an awning and at any rate far better than our wobbly garden parasol – with cake, coffee and brandy at our side, did a real conversation begin. All the more surprising, too, although surprising doesn't cover it.

"I've come direct from Palermo," he said, "the airport, well from Syracuse, a bit to the south, where we had our centre. Until now," he added after a mysterious pause.

We waited for him to continue. I bit into a big slice of the cake, which made it easier to modulate my reactions if need be. He had used the past tense; if he was about to tell us they were moving to New York, should we boil over with joy?

"We had a big ship, very big, in fact, making voyages in the Mediterranean with business people and academics on board. Newspaper people too. Initially, we rented it, for our first *Business Cruise,* but ended up buying it. To pursue new opportunities."

"You know, Carlos, we read about it," Madeleine threw in, all motherly smiles. "There was a big article in the *Financial Times*. About… *Roger*, wasn't it? After a king of Sicily?"

She must have googled that; our *Encyclopaedia Britannica*, 1980 edition, was still in Shurgard's hideaway together with the rest of our old household goods.

"Yes, *Roger the Second*," he said, without any great fanfare.

He had not so much as touched his cake, which may have been a bit burnt, but sipped frequently from his coffee and brandy.

"Our cruises got a good deal of publicity." A good deal of notoriety descending on yourselves didn't hurt, either, I thought.

"Anyway…" he continued, "we have defaulted."

A few resoundingly silent moments elapsed; about the time a skilled doctor needs to check your pulse.

If only intuitively sure about the nature of this catastrophe, Madeleine, covering her mouth, uttered a feeble moan, and I probably produced some sound too.

We had shared the same vague apprehensions without disclosing them to each other, not even when we talked about him. Besides, though we had assumed that the newspaper article was based on information provided by Carlos and his partners, we must in time have felt that what we had kept quiet about wasn't worth speaking of.

Carlos bent forward a couple of times and started rolling his shoulders as if he found his slatted chair uncomfortable, which it certainly was. But he had never had any problems with these chairs before; perhaps it was in preparation for what he was about to say next.

"It turned out differently from what we expected – differently from what we had good reason to expect. Eventually, we couldn't pay what we owed. Our cash flow wasn't enough."

We sat silent as mice: not much else we could do.

"Look, it isn't all doom and gloom," he said. "Terry's father, a shipbroker, has the economics of it well in hand. And I have an opportunity to reshape my prospects.

"I have had a fruitful meeting with Padre Piero in Palermo. He is, as you may know, a high-profile… You don't? He is a fairly well-known clergyman in Sicily, and I told him my story, all of it, without in any way reducing my own role or minimising my responsibility."

By now the sun had slid down enough to nibble at us through the cedar canopy. It is the proudest of trees around here, also the oldest and therefore with dry branches here and there, so we began to grope for our sunglasses. Carlos' were very dark, gold-rimmed and oversized, like those worn by President Truman. In what remained to be seen of his face, nothing particular could be read – neither bashfulness, nor relief, nor expectancy; nothing of any kind. At most, he had a dry mouth, since he was making those funny movements with cheeks and lips you make when in need of saliva.

A definite feeling of sympathy arose within me, if somewhat reluctantly, and in addition a kind of regard for his attitude. Yes, and why should he wear sackcloth and ashes when a matter-of-fact attitude, at bottom, seems much sounder?

"I wanted to make a clean breast," he said, "and Padre Piero gave me his… approval. His blessing."

*

Midnight. We had gone to bed an hour ago. Through the open window, the moon looked down on us so brightly that you could have read FT headlines by its light, even lead paragraphs. Well, not I, but Madeleine might.

Time and time again, a bird was calling, a raptor. A brown fish-owl, an extremely rare bird, native to tropical, humid Asia had been sighted at the derelict lighthouse not far from here by a party of British ornithologists, and we thought it might be that one. Interestingly, the male is smaller than the female. Madeleine put its calls on her bird sound recorder.

All of a sudden she was sitting on the edge of my bed.

"Are you awake?"

My eyes were closed but she knew I was. Otherwise, I wouldn't have been laying still on my back .This is what she used to say: *You are like a dog spinning round in his basket without ever coming to rest.*

"All of it is so strange. I'm so confused," she mumbled. "I don't even know how to start thinking about it."

"Yes," I mumbled back, in an even lower voice, after a moment adding, "can you imagine Carlos in a confessional?"

"Do you think his companions have tricked him?"

"Tricked or talked it over, who knows?"

"But he didn't try to exempt himself from responsibility, such a fine thing."

I shrugged, which she could both see and feel, as we were sitting so tightly together.

A different kind of question was distracting me. Carlos had been given some kind of exoneration by this Sicilian fellow. What for? As if default were a sin! How can a priest forgive sins anyway?

Funny, that people can think of such an idea. My God, how pretentious.

"Why did he seek pardon in the first place?" I said, my voice more than whispering now. "I should have been less surprised if he told us he's a transvestite."

A choked giggle escaped her. There was a scent of aloe vera from her hands.

"So instead of an insolvency judge, there is the Holy Spirit," I hissed.

She kissed me in the way she did at times; my cheeks, the

bridge of my nose and my mouth, in that order: "It's time for you to calm down, now. Ask Ivar if you don't believe me." He was resting on my bedside table in his knitted sleeping bag with green frogs on it.

I was granted permission to say one more thing: "Yet, it's you who are an atheist, not me. Confessional atheist even."

29

Next morning saw a rather low-key trio slouching out into the garden with their breakfast plates, taking up the same seats in front of the cedar as the day before.

A wonderful tree. Sometimes, its vanilla-like fragrance is almost overpowering; at other times, mild and eclipsed by the yellow half-tree, half-bush on the gable of our neighbour's house, which has a scent of jasmine without being one – often, when it's damp, as now, mixed with a smell of horse dung and beetroot, quite passable on ordinary days, from the compost further away.

We were not moving at the same speed. When Carlos was on his second cup of coffee, Madeleine was still to take her first, and I was in the middle of my yogurt and cereal. Carlos, gulping coffee with his left hand, was managing a mobile phone with the other; the generation of gadgets Madeleine and I are not familiar with, wafer thin.

It's not more than half past eight and the concrete mixers are already humming at full speed at the furthest end of the alley. Five more houses, larger than the others, and one overlooking the sea that we have declared an interest in buying. Every other day there are second thoughts, though.

"What are you up to?" asked Madeleine as if she suspected Carlos of booking a flight or a taxi to the airport.

"Oh, nothing really…"

He put the telephone down on the table, placing it between his almost empty plate – he wouldn't eat the purple pieces of fig – and a banana with a hard journey behind it, black as coal.

"I guess I forgot to tell you… I intend to do some voluntary work."

"Oh, is that so? What kind?" asked Madeleine.

"With Monsignor Piero, all kinds of work. For a year or so." He moved both palms vertically, like he was measuring out the period, then blew a couple of times on his coffee, which I had never seen him do before. Like Madeleine used to.

I was wondering whether he had intentionally divided what he wanted to communicate into two portions; one for yesterday, one for today. And what if he had? Our bedroom discussion came back to me with a vengeance; so it wasn't enough for him to go to confession; there had to be *penance*, too, *good works!* Well, I'll be damned…

I stroked my thumb right under my chin as I used to when I had a beard as a student, just stubble there now, sometimes several days' stubble, and turned towards Carlos. The chairs were too low for him, not really for me in spite of us being of about the same height. I said:

"It just struck me that the *Monsignor* – I don't know the English equivalent – might have been struggling to follow you? Given that his English skills might be poor, right? Or not a big deal, perhaps?"

Surprised as he may have been, he had neither an answer ready, nor a deadpan expression, as if playing a waiting game or something, and in fact I was groping around.

He knitted his brow a little, which was a good enough reaction for me to proceed.

"There are churches in Turkey too, you know. The Archdiocese of Izmir – you know Izmir, don't you – was visited by the pope some years ago. The one who was the first pope to resign, remember?"

He listened attentively now, as far as I could judge, but didn't say a word.

"So, I mean, if you wanted to confide in them – language no barrier – then your freedom of action…" my words coming out slowly, as if recited, "…might perhaps be affected differently, or not at all. You wouldn't have to tie your hands, no voluntary work, and so on," I wound up, and held my breath.

Dismissing my point or storing it somewhere underneath his well-cropped skull, no telling which, he got up after a while. "I have some business to attend to."

He put the mobile in one of the many zip pockets of his black trousers, and left.

We heard him pass the front gate. It is more of a decoration really, beautifully hand-wrought iron, which gives a twang when closing.

"Why should you bring up a new priest?" she asked. "Was that a constructive thing to do?"

"Yes, food for thought. Why not?"

"He might feel hurt."

"A default is bad news, okay, but to my mind a fact of business life, nothing disgraceful or outrageous – I pledge my subscription to the *Financial Times* – unless it was done in bad faith. And certainly not a *sin*."

A dissatisfied pause. Then I continued:

"It's for a judge or such like to handle, not for a priest or his buddy the Holy Spirit to sneak into."

"Now look, Birger, don't forget Carlos wanted it. He wanted to see a priest. We can't sit in judgement over his feelings."

Of course, she had a point.

I had excited myself – even had to take off my t-shirt,

something a real Turk would hesitate to do. Sympathies with Carlos or not, the church connection was sickening. The difference between Madeleine and I was probably that her mixture of feelings was founded on sadness, whereas mine on annoyance, and not really over Carlos, the target being much wider.

"The oddest thing of all," I said, no doubt quite acidly, "as if it were not enough with the blessing, he is to be exploited, too, labour for them for free. Burning his bridges in the process."

This didn't work with Madeleine at all.

"You don't know if he will be paid or not."

"Oh yes, I know what voluntary work means."

I wiped my armpits with the t-shirt.

"It comes down to this: he buys himself free from sin, from something that doesn't even exist, and pays for it with his labour at a giveaway price."

At fever pitch as I was, I may not have noticed that this was an unnecessary rerun. Or was this rather my way of lamenting her lack of attention?

"I told you, *paying* is neither here nor there. He feels gratitude!"

"Priests are *sin freaks!* Without this traffic in sin, they would lose half of their money, half of their work too, just marriages and baptisms left. No wonder they won't easily come up with a modern view. And funerals, I forgot those, in the name of fairness: funerals too."

"Hush," she said, and shook the five spread fingers of her right hand at me, like when holding a handball.

"Hush? No one around here would understand," I said.

"Oh yes, Fatosh would. And *you-know-who* would both understand and circulate it among her school colleagues that you are shouting, which you don't usually do, and at a high pitch too.

"Besides, why this sermonising? Do I need it?"

"Sermonising? Okay, I will calm down." But damned quick I revved up again.

"Commercially speaking, their ethics fall far short of today's standards. Their Mystery Line supplies beliefs, absolution included. But do they present a product label, plain and true, to the sinners, their clients? No, that's part of the small print: *We priests are only bound by our holy beliefs, no guarantee included,*" I added in an unctuous voice.

"Label? Guarantee or not, what's the difference!"

"It makes all the difference in the world. Carlos is buying a pig in a poke, doesn't even know for sure that his iniquities are being washed away. And then he is to gracefully give away his labour to the church. If that isn't exploitation, I don't know what is. And the priest, what about his efforts – producing added value or not?"

With fresh roses on her tanned cheeks, Madeleine took the empty water pitcher from the table to go inside, but turned on the threshold:

"Now put on your t-shirt. Fatosh is coming for me."

She returned with the pitcher rattling with ice cubes. Smiling vaguely, she seemed intent on not letting her cheeks flower again.

"You have really become business-minded all of a sudden, haven't you?"

I had no answer to that.

"What's *added value*?" she asked. "Or is it *value added*?"

"I didn't know it myself until I started with the *Financial Times*," I said mildly. "The reason why bankers are so frequently dissed is that we don't benefit from them – zero value added. Bankers and priests are in the same boat."

"I hope you won't speechify like this where Carlos can hear."

"Of course not. This was, just for you, a special treat."

"Do you suppose I haven't heard most of your sermons

before?" she said in a kindly tone.

I came to her side and kissed the tip of her nose while pinching her nasal root, like some birds do when mating. I have never seen it but Madeleine has described it to me.

"And please, don't try to pick holes in him. And no gags. It's no easy thing for him to distinguish between your humour and serious intent. I can barely manage it myself."

"So I went too far just now?"

"What's the meaning of it? Why should your ideas on the church be imposed on Carlos?"

"Not just mine, yours too, and what I said was meant to be of use to him. Potential use."

"Birger, he is worth better than mockery, don't you think?"

"Quite so. Yes, of course. The scorn is for the priests."

"I told you – if he is all the better for it, how can we be against it?"

I nodded in agreement. As the weather forecast for us had improved, I felt like pouring a last bucket of oil on residual waves.

"That he is willing to do voluntary work may be a very good sign, perhaps, though I would never have guessed he had a taste for it."

Or the talent, I thought, but not out loud.

*

I dreamed Madeleine was pestering me: *You should* say *sorry!* To whom and for what, she wouldn't say.

No, I said. *No*.

Why not?

Vakitsiz öten horozun bashini keserler! I had in mind to translate: *There's a proper time for everything*, but didn't bother as she was already preparing a reply.

So, the cock that cries too early gets his head chopped off? Is that what you say? Spirited, but no less stupid for it.

I felt terrible.

I don't believe dreams mean anything. Was that crazy cock on the go again last night? That's how far my interpretation of dreams goes.

30

"I hear your son is back," said Zia.

The news network operates fast here, about as quickly as the grocer's tongue. Hotty's too, I imagine. Both put social media to shame.

"He is back, yes," I answered, somewhat half-heartedly.

Zia stacked my mail on the counter, a medium-sized heap, and put it in a plastic bag. As usual there were mostly the pink FT newspapers, including a thick issue of *How to Spend It* inserted in a weighty Saturday-Sunday issue. Fingers crossed he hadn't taken a peak at it.

In spite of the smoking prohibition issued some years ago, it still reeked of cigarette smoke in the lobby and, according to Madeleine, even our mail stinks. An upholsterer would have a tough job making this room decent. The portrait of Atatürk staring into the sky, himself an avid smoker, had been temporarily taken off the wall, leaving behind a large rectangular shadow and a big brass screw.

At this time of the year, and the day, the only window there, behind the counter, gave a view of a cloudy sky and two mountain slopes with a grassy but stony flatland between them, one draped in mist, the other with black and green patches after last year's fires.

I found it important to correct Zia: "You know, Carlos, he isn't my son."

He didn't sway his head, politely agreeing as he otherwise used to do, but opened his mouth.

"Ha!"

This is an interesting Turkish word, one of many with elusive meanings and lacking a one-word equivalent in English. Out of Zia's mouth it had come truncated and rather hoarsely.

"What do you mean? You told me so yourself," he said.

"Well…" I shook my head, and his answer to this was to light a cigarette.

We marched out to the honeysuckle-ensnared portico. In fact, the owner of the hotel doesn't approve of Zia's smoking there, either, and never in front of guests or visitors. I, of course, consider myself to be neither.

"It's high time to get things in order," he said. "It can't go on like this."

Obscure though these words might have seemed to others, they were crystal clear to me.

"Believe me, Zia, I can't possibly disagree with you – but I am not someone who can bring it up with him."

"Ha! Tell him I want to talk to him." Zia was screwing up his dark brown eyes, a semaphore signal of discomfort, either with the smoke or, God forbid, with me. He had been losing hair recently, and in two years, if this continued, he would be bald as a pumpkin and wrinkled as a desiccated fig.

"Absolutely, yes. But…" I said, drawing a deep breath.

"I put my trust in you."

"As I told you, I have no sway with him. None at all."

I felt like saying something snappy in Turkish: *It is easier to make a camel jump a ditch than to make a fool listen to reason*, but hesitated too long.

If there is one man in this remote region that I consider to be more than an acquaintance, a friend, it is Zia. Well, on second thoughts, there is Abdullah too.

"You should have told me," he said.

I left but after some distance, I turned around. The hotel stood there like a still life, like a *baklava* with mint leaves against a background of grey gauze. I raised my free hand in the air in some kind of salute if it should happen he was still there. At this time of the day, a crooked old woman used to herd her goats across the field to the pasture up in the valley; a restful view and sometimes a nice chat too, but there was no sign of her, either.

*

It was basically a matter of packaging; I was strongly leaning towards a casual version: *Oh, I came across Zia the other day. What a smoker he is. A pity, really. His skin takes a beating. Have you noticed? By the way, Carlos, he wanted a chance to see you – or, not that – a chance to say hallo.*

I hadn't had time to polish it when, at breakfast, Madeleine prompted me: "You had something to tell Carlos?" It took him as unawares as it did me.

As she knows, I'm only fictitiously up and about until I've had my morning coffee, so she might have waited a little; but then Carlos was almost finished with his. I related my discussion with Zia as best I could, with conflicting feelings; imagine a cat finding ants in its food bowl.

Half way through, Carlos crossed his arms and looked down at the tablecloth, which certainly was worthy of admiration – antique and handwoven, floral Ottoman decor, which Carlos didn't know, of course, and given to us by Abdullah just before our first trip to India.

When I had finished talking, for way too long and haltingly, Carlos let his hands fall down on his thighs with a smack. "Thanks for letting me know," he said, ending with a sound resembling a sigh, which it might well have been.

We let the silence speak for a moment, waiting for him to continue. But no. I doubted I could urge him to say more; you can't get blood out of a stone.

*

Madeleine's concern and mine were not exactly the same.

"Carlos, losing this beautiful cruiser," she asked, "will you get over it?"

"First, we were not really the owners. Second, we are not at the end of the line, so not to worry."

He gave her a good-natured smile; whether it was completely genuine is another matter, and she reciprocated, although without much of her bunny teeth showing.

"I'm at a milestone right now," he continued. "Considering an investment in my future. Goes without saying that opportunity costs of varying kinds will have to be measured. But, you see, historical costs don't come into it. On the contrary, those are always a fallacy."

"I'm glad you are not unhappy. You don't look so."

Had I understood the meaning of his words, *historical costs*, it was only by a hair's breadth. Don't grieve over spilt milk – that was my guess, no telling, of course, if also Madeleine's. Anyway, she didn't appear nonplussed at all, and while asking a new question, she seemed quite free and easy, light of heart; and even half nonchalant, half appreciative.

"Now, this voluntary work with the priest, you are not burning your bridges, are you?"

He shook his head. "You see, an economist has to consider *externalities*, in particular *positive externalities*, of course, as simple as that," he said, moving his eyes from Madeleine to me for an unknown reason. I felt as if under scrutiny. I probably was, and hoped there wasn't much to catch.

"This is a must. A *sine qua non* for any company," he added, his attention swinging back and forth between both of us now. "It comes with the expectations inherent in the business function."

Did he have something complicated to say, or was it that he wanted it to seem so? *Financial Times* subscriber as I was, I couldn't tell.

"But... but you have no company any longer!"

"Oh yes, I have! Any competent MBA, whether or not integrated into a wider structure, is a business company in his own right."

"Aha."

"And obviously," he continued, "your personality management has spillover effects, so see to it that they are *positive* rather than *negative*. With Monsignor, they will be quite positive. I expect no less." He wound up his point with a self-satisfied smile.

Was this *econo-gobbledegook* invented by himself or picked up from elsewhere? Either way, I couldn't grasp how it was related to conscience and penitence. I would have thought that if you have asked a priest to absolve you, without being a member of his church, it is because you have hit rock bottom. But that was not the impression he gave. Or was it just a show, just to thumb his nose at me? Yet, it was Madeleine who had put the question. She looked unperturbed.

"It's so nice to have you here," she said.

He smiled, by my reckoning the third this visit.

"Is it to get a good rest?" she continued. "Unless you have a particular purpose?"

I was glad of these questions, as they were firmly rooted in my own thoughts. Whereas I always had to fish carefully for information, Madeleine's circumstances were naturally quite different.

"Yes, I needed a break," he said. "And then I wanted to tell you all this, about what I am engaged in."

"Good," said Madeleine, approvingly, and then as if it had just sprang to mind, "what does it all mean for Elif? Will she go back home, to living with her parents?"

She didn't mention Zia's name, I noted. Good. Just as well.

"I don't know. There's no deal," he said.

Madeleine did not seem to understand, and his bland countenance gave no clue. "No deal?"

"Yes. It isn't as if we have one, you see." But he added: "Yet."

I, like Madeleine, judging from the slight twist of her upper lip, was not comfortable with his choice of words. You couldn't help wondering… Used between two lovers, wasn't such a word – deal – in itself likely to break a deal rather than make one? It left a bad taste in my mouth.

"In any case, if you wish to speak to Zia, Birger could be your translator."

I gave a nod. Okay, I would do it.

"His English is really tricky," I said, well aware that Carlos thought so, "no doubt about it."

In an amateurish wind-up of my servility, I added: "Funnily enough, it's easier to understand his English if you happen to know some Turkish."

"And I don't," said Carlos.

I strongly regretted not keeping my mouth shut. On reflection, I would have preferred not to get drawn into this at all. Zia was probably expecting him to ask for Elif's hand. And now Carlos might even be sending her packing. I wouldn't assist with translating something like that.

It suddenly came to me. When Carlos arrived here the first time, beginning his excursions along the Turkish coast, our car was at his disposal, but he used it only initially, a couple of times, no more. Yet it was close at hand and always ready; he didn't even have to think about filling up the tank. How come he hadn't been keen to use this home comfort? The reason was there right under my nose. He wouldn't risk bumping into Zia.

I started to feel even stronger discomfort, physical even. Like my skin was shrinking, and spiders or bugs or something were crawling all over my body. In my hair, all over me. And this feeling pushed me far out to the verge of aggression.

Your nonchalance, Carlos, your negligence! That Zia will take out on me. Am I to lose my best or only friend here for someone who is definitely less than my friend, who flies into a tantrum at the mere thought of someone mistaking me for his father? Which, I can tell you I'm damned happy not to be!

I had told Zia that I'd washed my hands of Carlos, which he didn't like to hear, while Carlos more than anyone else would love to hear it. And, truth be told, I possess no power over either of them.

*

When young, did I play it straight myself? I don't think I came out of my amorous adventures morally unscathed. Besides, I can only guess at what the cards are in Carlos' hand; he may have offered her the prospect of an idyllic future together – or he may not. He may have been completely frank, offering nothing – taking things one day at a time. His fault lies in being ignorant or negligent of her cultural circumstances. Also on that count I may have been his like. So, who am I to bridle at Carlos? Am I one to lecture another on the propriety of his sentiments?

Why behold you the speck that is in your brother's eye, but consider not the beam that is in your own eye? So says the Bible! Which, however, is far behind the times. To be sure I see a beam in my eye, but that doesn't diminish his. Or does it?

31

In the mornings, at this time of year, dark blue clouds can gather above the sea, growing rapidly and finally blotting out the horizon. But this gloomy curtain can later transform into pale cloud puffs that go sailing restively in the sky. For weeks, it starts like this, and it is difficult to tell how the day is going to be, but generally the sun comes out triumphantly before noon. We may not have appreciated its victory to the full, though, as we were locked in Carlos' mess.

Directly after breakfast, Madeleine would hurry away in her red one-piece for a swim, hurrying back up the stairs at an even greater speed, if possible, and her bathing suit nearly dry. Then she prepared her courses – exercise therapy with music – and so she was shuffling around in the living room accompanied by Harry Belafonte and similar soft tunes.

Carlos, with a rekindled relationship with his silvery laptop, was encamped under the cedar, close to the trunk where he had moved a chair and an old rickety flowerpot table dug out from the garden shed and which, precisely because of its instability, could be forcefully tamed to take up a steady position in among the intricate network of surface roots.

He produced a continuous tapping, which was accompanied by the chirruping of big-ego grasshoppers, with a break every half an hour or so to sit staring at his fingernails or flex his shoulders, or else grab roasted nuts from little sacks under the table.

My place was rather on the periphery, where I was shaded by an LGBT-striped parasol in an overly heavy concrete stand (good for your arm muscles). With a deep lack of concentration, I was reading reports from Jens – financial reports, market strategies, organisational matters, what have you; reading stuff like this does not come easy, never did.

There were letters, too, from both known and unknown people that needed some thinking about, including some begging letters. One also from a great joker from faraway in my past, who in lieu of his name on the back of the envelope had written *Sicilia insula est* – the first words in our first Latin book. An invitation to a class reunion?

Both of us were casually dressed, shorts and sweatshirts, but whereas I was barefoot, Carlos had his blue metallic runners on – textile but glimmering – and wore his baseball cap backwards. Working better as a thinking cap that way? Who knows; I gave him the benefit of the doubt.

There was nothing conspicuous about me, at least if you shut your eyes to my legs, more and more hairy every year. Or my long toenails, what with my stiff back, or these days senility cum laziness, if there is such a thing.

In the beginning, I thought Carlos was writing emails in a never-ending stream, a sizeable number since there was nothing which needed printing. Then, after a few days, I got the strong impression – could be on account of the rhythm of the keyboard clatter – that he wasn't chat-scrawling but writing more advanced texts and perhaps using advanced materials such as graphics or big data, which required him from time to time to get fresh batteries or memory or whatever it was from his room.

He seemed to be out of the doldrums now; a great deal more aplomb than only a few days earlier.

Much as I liked my garden chair, padded and kind to my back, I found it trying now and felt a frequent, insistent urge to stretch my legs. Of course I had to avoid coming over as a snooper, which wasn't a very easy thing, as the cedar was in the middle of everything. I moved as if a four-metre area around him was taped off.

I left the house for saunters in the neighbourhood – meandering a little as a matter of precaution lest I find myself trapped by someone, such as the Captain in his glossy cap with a gold strap, who might tax my patience; not much civility left in the reserve tank, I feared.

I liked to walk without an aim, winding my way around the hotel skeletons, which would probably remain just that: skeletons with no prospect of having flesh on their bones. Madeleine says she prefers the aspect of pure decay, of something that has at least had a meaningful existence, to the grisly view of a bag of bones.

I wasn't relaxed enough to pause in my tracks to see distracting things around me, which I otherwise may have done, like the puddles there with beautiful spotted frogs that jumped up as soon as you put down your foot on the edges of them.

I swapped these walks for runs up and along the eastern, less steep mountain slope, but overdid it, stumbling badly and hurting my foot. In fact, I wonder if it is training – intended to keep myself in trim – that is causing my ailments, rather than age.

With three Turkish dailies in the backpack, I took the bus to Antalya instead after this happened. A long trip it was but well worth it, and finally I found myself at Migros, the grand shopping mall at the end of Atatürk Boulevard. The hubbub inside this cornucopia of more than one hundred establishments paradoxically offsets my inner commotion.

I set course for the big book shop and came out with a

thin volume on probability theory – *Bayles Theorem* sounded interesting – and an equally slim volume of poetry by Nazim Hikmet, relieved myself of my unread newspapers, and headed for my favourite café, Shakespeare Bistro.

In spite of its name, I may have been the only customer reading poetry, but with Turks you never know.

For once, I would enjoy cappuccino made *lege artis* (sorry, medical jargon), so it would be done properly. I ground two antacids and threw in a third when I ordered a second cup. The more I looked into the Hikmet book and the more life-giving coffee I sipped, the better my mood became.

> 'Living is no joke,
> you must live with great seriousness,
> like a squirrel for instance…'

These lines I liked a lot but as I continued reading, I came to understand it wasn't a humorous piece at all, on the contrary, and set the book aside.

I may have a declining sense of duty towards Carlos, I mused, but I do have a strong feeling of solidarity with Madeleine. And the only way for me to be useful now is through money.

It wasn't as if I had put any effort into exploiting my findings myself. I hadn't – Madeleine had done all that, and worked hard on me to ensure I did not miss the boat. Hence, I had suggested that Jens transfer half of my liquid assets to her, but she had always opposed this. Well, regardless, I would ask Jens to do it, and that's that. As it involves Carlos too, she might accept it; and she would be free to offer him money or guarantees, or whatever, with money from her own pocket.

*

"You said *default*, what does it mean?"

Since it was Madeleine who had asked this question, Carlos could not assume there was a hidden agenda in it. Economics were not her cup of tea, and she wasn't the least bit embarrassed to show it.

"What does it mean? It's all a matter of cash, and we didn't have enough to carry on."

"But you were going to get an enormous sum of money for your cruiser. They wrote about it…"

"Right, but the regulators intimated that they would review the rules of the game."

Rules of the game? I thought.

"*Regulators*?" said Madeleine.

"Exactly," he said emphatically. "Very zealous chaps that are set up to police entrepreneurs. Particularly in the EU and the USA, manipulating rules wantonly – and particularly on bookkeeping. Our partners – we had business with big companies all over the world, which need to upgrade their executives… This upset their human resource planning and then they became much more hesitant to make bookings with us. So there we are."

"Others been hurt too?" Madeleine asked.

"Certainly, companies with similar profiles. Some for good reason, perhaps."

"In your case, I mean, other than you and your two partners?"

"Well," he said, "it's true that some of those who supported us along the way have been affected. We launched a pre-IPO, you see." No, the truth was we didn't see, but perhaps that wasn't necessary, either. "And some investors were hit," he added, shrugging it off. You may let your shoulders do the talking in many situations, even a deplorable situation. I understood.

Madeleine gave a long sigh: "Ooh!"

After a moment, she said, almost voiceless: "Are you in hot

water now? On the wrong side of the law?"

"No, no, no police or judges or anything like that. As I say, Terry's father has it all in hand."

I couldn't sit thin-lipped any longer: "What does he do, anyway? Is he a lawyer?"

"Well, yes, he is," Carlos replied, raising his eyebrows at my knowing this, or guessing right. I had done neither; just a prompt it was, and I seemed to remember Carlos telling me he was a shipbroker.

Madeleine asked him: "Do you have debts?" A good question, indeed, and I envy her forthright ways. Or should one say: forthright when she wants to be?

"It won't come to that. Terry's father wouldn't like to see his son in debt," he said, and gave Madeleine a blink or something; I didn't quite see it before he had started to nod reassuringly.

While Carlos and Madeleine continued talking about his company, and what might have been, I felt an urge to sort my importunate feelings, if not suspicions. Still, I heard occasional phrases – "selling shares in our company"... "recuperate it" (the cruiser?)... "Milan stock exchange." Fragments like these. And I heard him raise his voice a notch: "Davos, but not in the Alps, on the sea!"

Was it that the regulators had considered their cruises more like relaxation for the participants than executive training? As fringe benefits liable to tax? If so, that was likely to turn the tables, of course, or the office desks, so to speak.

But, if bookkeeping rules are susceptible to change, as he said, shouldn't they have reckoned on that? No anticipation? No warning?

To whom will they turn for support now? Not difficult to guess, right? A pity I threw the newspaper article away; however, an Egyptian shipbroking company planned to buy their boat, and the father of Carlos' partner is Egyptian and a shipbroker;

yeah, quite so. According to the newspaper, the sale was part of a structural reorganisation or something, which suggests that these three guys were in a tight corner even then.

So, how much will it cost this Terry's father? Or perhaps rather his company, and would he be willing to get involved just like that? Will he put the clamps on Carlos? That's what I would like to know.

32

A little dog is peeking around the corner. I know full well who this is – her natural eyeliners make even belly dancers green with envy. After a moment's hesitation, she starts to lumber slowly towards me until she comes to a halt a bit to my left with a little plump.

Carlos and I had both taken our usual places at the back of the house, I having moved just a bit away from the terrace.

It was a lovely morning, the sky a bit overcast, comfortably hot and not really humid, mild perfumes flowing from all directions; heather, pomegranates and peaches fallen from the trees, spoiled watermelons… Everything around our house is wasteland, so it's free, or considered so, for whoever wants it. This year, Fatosh has expanded *her* cultivation area behind the metal-clad pump house and made holes for banana suckers. An interesting experiment.

"*Merhaba*," I exclaimed.

Carlos turned his head in my direction: "Shoo it away!"

Addressing both of them, I replied: "She lives here. More or less."

In fact, less. I have given her food – she likes cornflakes and potato – several times, picked her up, too. Her neck and ears smell of… I don't know what, perhaps toasted gluten-free bread and roasted almonds.

Looking away from the dog, staring just at me, his Truman glasses off, he said: "What do you mean? You haven't bought it, I suppose?"

"Not really, it's more like we have found each other… She is *Sabhia*."

She was named on the spur of the moment and I was going to add: *After Atatürk's daughter, who, you know, became a fighter pilot*, but stopped myself at the last moment. Did he even know that Atatürk was the founder of modern Turkey?

"They have rabies, don't they? And you are required by law to vaccinate?"

There I was with my pants down.

"I don't know."

"Hi," I said to Sabhia.

She wagged her tail, as she would whatever I might say in that tone of voice, then yawned, not out of sleepiness to be sure.

Interestingly, human beings make a good deal of noise when drawing in air and then pushing it out, whereas dogs do not. Sabhia, even though yawning with her mouth wide open and her tongue rolled out, did so inaudibly, except for a small click at the end of the performance, like when you shut a well-made jewellery case.

"Damn filthy. And lousy, no doubt."

Words were not needed to tell me this; his revulsion was quite clear from his fleshy grimace.

Admittedly, she looked a bit *unwashed*. Yet there must be someone looking after her – at times, if not always – as her fur wasn't shaggy.

"Look at its tail!" he snorted.

"Yea, charming, isn't it?"

"Like an *L*, upside down," he said. Then emphatically: "It's broken."

"Well, I've seen it like an *I* and an *S* too."

I couldn't help adding: "Wouldn't surprise me if she could even make a *Z*."

He put on his sunglasses – threw them on – and turned back to his computer screen, clattering away more forcefully now than before, I thought, but I might have been mistaken.

I picked up Sabhia. I brought her nose to my ear as if it were a telephone receiver, just for her to display a little affection, a lick perhaps. In vain. The line was dead, and wisely so. Why would she get herself involved in our disharmony?

33

A Turkish-made car of yore – branded Falcon, a bit ruffled but far from wing-broken – came at high speed and braked hard in front of our gate.

Sitting in the backseat was the Dutchwoman, keeping a close eye on a large roasting pan at her side, with a slow- cooked leg of mutton for us to feast upon on the terrace – as a special treat for Carlos, and, in fact, Mr Hotty's idea.

The dusk was deepening, frogs and crickets all full of beans. Funny that such small creatures can be so noisy. Madeleine heard nightjars too, but I couldn't make them out.

Carlos started talking about the future, his future. Under his own power; we didn't even have to coax him with questions.

"Ah, things have become much clearer," he explained. If his heart was surging now, it was thanks to his sleek silver laptop rather than to us. Nor to the dinner, I thought, although there was plenty of savoury meat and rich red wine (Australian Shiraz, sixteen percent), and he was certainly relishing both. There was far more food than three servings and we fell upon it with wolfish appetite after our physical exercise earlier in the day – Madeleine, alone in the water, had been breaststroking across the bay for more than an hour. All of the mutton slipped down so easily, the dessert too, Turkish pistachio *baklavas*, very sweet and baked by Mr Hotty himself.

It was in the middle of all this that Madeleine said just what I had been fearing all along, and hoping she wouldn't say, at least not before consulting with me.

"Carlos, you know of course you can stay with us as long as you want. Whenever you want."

Now she had done it. Well, that would certainly take some getting used to. All right, then we'll have to weigh up moving into something bigger. Much bigger. As a last resort. But under no circumstances would I move out of Liman, not willing to alter my present way of living.

Simplicity, incommodity if you like, and peacefulness, have been a help to me, are indeed a help for those of my sort. And unspoilt nature. In the mountains around here there are still less than two disposable plastic bottles per kilometre.

"Thank you," Carlos said, stroking Madeleine's shoulder.

He was sitting close to her, and I opposite them. Not only had his plans become clearer, but his face also had a different aspect. Although he was still young with no wrinkles, it was as if he was smoothed out somehow. Perhaps he had gained a little weight, or else it was just my imagination.

"I have now completed my career as a co-director of a rather successful enterprise," Carlos said, "although the returns did not match projections."

He had certainly drunk half of the wine. Under the influence of it? In fact, a great deal more than half, Madeleine had had less than a glass and I only a thimbleful. Had I known it was going to be a big festive occasion, which after a while it promised to be, a family celebration of sorts, then I would certainly have disregarded my grouchy gastric mucosa.

"I'm not one to sit on my hands. Next, I mean to go into asset management, tapping into new markets, in fact, into the *Christian* market, which has a huge potential."

"How do you mean, potential?"

"Churches have assets, you see, and there are over half a billion Christians in Europe alone who have assets as well," he said, radiating calm and confidence, just like when I saw him giving instructions at that computer simulation session.

"Many are in need of guidance and we will provide financial advice and management. Along Christian lines. Suggesting financial products, all kinds, including a healthy dose of *venture* capital that unfortunately many have heard described as 'ugly' in the media and elsewhere. We have a mission to fulfil."

In my head, I could not keep quiet: *Yea, becoming part of the church's mission.* I have a knack for irony and sarcasm. Harmless on the whole, as I seldom use it, but keep it to myself. Sometimes, though, a piercing weapon, if threatened, or if somebody resorts to improper arguments. And, perhaps, when I find myself at a disadvantage.

Madeleine asked: "What does venture capital mean?"

"It's when you move savings to placements with a high return but which presumably are a bit riskier. Very high, sometimes. Risk is of course always amalgamated with savings, like peas and carrots, sort of."

He had said *we*, so I asked:

"And will you continue to work with your earlier partners?"

"Still in the balance. They will have an Islamic profile. *Sukuk*, you know. But a couple of years on, some coordination may develop. If so, it will be *ecumenical asset management,* so to speak."

And he was smiling – for the fourth time, according to my reckoning, and I was included in it – chuckling too.

So this was the chuckle of the CEO of the *Good Shepherd Hedge Fund,* I thought, *so to speak.* The idea was odd to say the least. As Islam abhors lending at interest, this sharia-friendly thing called *sukuk* had been invented – that I knew from the *Financial Times.* But what would Christian values translate into: *Turn the Other Cheek* investments?

Was there even a need to contrive something, as Christians are probably no different from other people when it comes to money?

Being concerned with Carlos' future, or cutting loose from it, had almost become a full-time job – at least if including Madeleine's preoccupations too. And where had it brought us? I could fancy Carlos gliding across the floors of old Sicilian sanctuaries, swinging a censer, sprinkling holy water around, and none the better for it.

34

We hear someone scraping his shoes on the entrance stone.

Every now and then at this hour, neighbours pop in; those who think they know me well enough to ask for a prescription show me an infected finger wound or something. These visits are a bit awkward, as they so easily lead to queries beyond my expertise: pneumonia, angina, what have you. None of that now.

"Come in," Madeleine calls out, "I've printed it all off."

Together with Fatosh, she is to visit garden centres the following day and has googled for catalogues. Easy to mail them, of course, but after all it's only 30 metres between our houses.

Dinner had just ended and we were lingering at the big dining room table, leafing through newspapers and magazines while our cappuccinos were being prepared by the espresso machine bought in North Cyprus not so long ago. Fully automated *Rising Sun*, a pirate copy, reliable but slow.

Madeleine and Carlos were seated opposite each other below the large faïence dishes in glaring colours –woman with amphora, flowering meadow, not antique *maiolica*, as one might believe, but 20th century Swedish.

I was furthest from the wall and thus the first to notice that we were mistaken. It wasn't Fatosh, but Zia.

Immediately I got up, but as we were shaking hands, he sort of shoved me back down again with his left hand, which I accepted, having a strong feeling what this was all about. Carlos too? I could hear him muttering *festoon* or *balloon*, or was it *buffoon*? I couldn't trust my ears.

Zia placed both hands on the rail of the nearest chair, and so with us in front of him, bobbing a little on his feet as if standing behind a lectern. All right then, I mused, just as well. Or perhaps not.

Zia has a slender build but you perceive him as strong and definitely muscular, with biceps that may not look very impressive when viewed from the front, but are so much more so viewed from the side as, presumably, the shorter head on the inside of the arm is not really engaged in his daily work. Wearing a jade-coloured shirt makes him appear darker than he is; in fact, I never saw him in anything but bright shirts. His face, today more than ever, does not match the youthful physique.

In Turkish, he says: "Our families need to talk," and pulls out a couple of handwritten notes from his breast pocket.

"Should have happened sooner, of course," he adds with a friendly tilt of the end, this time in English. "Both families may have been *unenterprising*." He stumbles on the pronunciation.

Zia has been gifted with a friendly countenance, as if naturally smiling, although you couldn't pin down with certainty where in his face this mien has its domicile, whether in the thin lips, curved upwards, or somewhere in the network of his many wrinkles, if you choose to see them in that way.

Family – Zia had uttered this word twice. Not one to Carlos' liking, as I well knew, but he should realise by now that Zia uses it as a matter of course, and with a meaning that is not necessarily the same as for us, whatever that is.

By the way, is Elif in on this? I didn't want to challenge Zia by asking; now was certainly not the right moment to question the commission he had given himself.

"Had I known how things would turn out, I would not have let her go," he continued, again in English.

That he would willingly bring down a language handicap on himself, I mused. Generous; more than generous in a situation like this.

"As I know and respect your father, there was no need for me to exact a promise from you."

Carlos sat motionless and looked out through the space between me and Madeleine, seemingly captivated by something on the other side of the glass wall, as if lost in reverie. A benign interpretation that Zia surely wouldn't buy, would he?

"In Italy, you have been living together as man and wife. Am I wrong?" He pointed with his index finger, but not exactly at anything in particular, curved as it was, just held it up in the air.

Carlos could say yes or no, I thought; that wasn't much to ask. Of course, it would have been stupid, more than stupid for me to try to address him and stare him into it. I can't work on him in that way; in fact, in no way that I know of.

Madeleine was sitting silent. I knew she had hoped for a restful afternoon. In the morning, she had gone down to the beach. Black lumps drifting around, Caretta caretta. Her eczema makes her go through fire and water if necessary. No wit intended.

"Now… here and now, we will settle a schedule."

At first, his words had come out slowly from a pursed mouth; he was groping his way with frequent pauses. But he gradually found his feet. Even if he had been assisted with the translation into English, which he must have been, this was a feat, a show of stamina, zeal and strength. Yes, he was certainly strong for his sixty years, if a bit worn on the outside.

Suddenly it appeared to me that the woman's head covering the earthenware dish above Carlos' head actually bore a striking similarity to Elif – beautifully brown, high cheekbones, bushy eyebrows. Did Zia see that? Or was he too stuck in his notes to make such an observation?

"The schedule can be changed if justified, but not just like that. The most important thing is the date."

Carlos was sitting just as he had been doing all the time, only now he had begun rocking his training-shoe-clad foot up and down; I couldn't see it but the vibrations on the wooden floor told me. Nor were his eyes stable, but from what I could judge, they never wandered in Zia's direction.

Zia's presentation was more fluent now and his voice had gained force, suddenly reaching a much higher pitch too:

"And this will be announced!"

It was like singing *Send him victorious* after *God save the queen*, minus the fanfare, perfect 5th, trained for it while in a boys' choir. Equally suddenly he was back on the former pitch:

"Finally then, let me know your convenient days."

While the note he had leaned on so far was merely a sheet from a notebook, the second that he was now unfolding was A4-size and contained his entire programme, I assumed. He had not exactly gone easy on us, but not unfriendly, either, I thought, and now for someone from our family, perhaps? And time for all parties to show conciliation.

As Zia carefully smoothed out the sheet with his hand, the conversation turned, although not in the way he might have anticipated, or Madeleine or I, either, for that matter. Madeleine had not uttered a word, and nor had I, if you exclude my body language, which hopefully had spoken volumes.

I had looked into his face as often as my neck permitted for moral support – telling him I wasn't the one to speak against him, just as I had told him earlier – tried to –during the conversation we had in the hotel lobby, or wherever it was.

My gaze was redirected to Carlos. Without turning a hair, he rose to his feet. And while so doing, said, as if in passing:

"To tell the truth, I'm up to here with it now." He then started doing shoulder rolls behind his chair. "If there is something more he has to get off his chest, he can do it somewhere else. He owns a phone, as far as I know, and so does Elif." He moved a bit further away from the table to allow more space for his exercises, with total indifference, real or simulated, as to how he came across.

Oh God, what is coming now?

Zia was at a loss – the flesh of his brown face stretched a bit more taut than usual, or was it just the play of the sunlight, its last rays of the day slanting down from just above the jagged mountain crest, flowing in through the glass wall? Maybe Zia hadn't understood him, or maybe he had; either way, I decided to step in, awkward though it was, given a responsibility that I in my heart of hearts doubted I had.

"Well," I said, attracting Zia's attention. "It would appear to me that Carlos means…" I was struggling to find words.

Zia's dilated but unblinking eyes looked at me like two black wood-knots.

"Carlos means, I think, that Elif herself should perhaps have a chance to discuss…"

Still searching for words – should I say discuss this matter or discuss their future or… I saw out of the corner of my eye Carlos coming closer to the glass wall.

The next second there was a gentle rattle from the beaded, flamingo-patterned door curtain and I didn't catch more than a glimpse of his left shoe disappearing through the parting and the pink flamingo flapping slowly.

Zia immediately read my stupefaction and in a twinkling of an eye he was off after him.

Stunned, as if incapacitated, Madeleine and I remain seated, unable to rouse ourselves. What could we do other than sit on the edge of our seats and listen, pricking up our ears?

A shrill voice in the distance shouted *Stop* a couple of times, or rather: *Dur! Dur!* – not English any longer.

A feral hog is not to be trifled with.

"Are you worried?" I asked Madeleine. Strangely, with a dimmed voice.

"Yes."

I reach out for her hand.

No use his fleeing. Most paths behind the houses go through stony thickets and across small, long abandoned plantations with rusty barbed wire and fallen fence posts here and there, some ending blindly. Rough going, literally on Zia's own ground.

The evening was closing in and the stars as well as the mast on the ridge started twinkling at us. If only in modest shape, the moon was there too, a thin crescent no bigger than that on top of the minaret, struggling to throw a shy light down the mountainside.

*

In Zia's breast, I guessed, had raged a war between conflicting strong feelings and sympathy for me having drawn the short straw. At least he hadn't turned on me, against me, I mean.

To Carlos, the temptation to laugh Zia off had become overwhelming, apparently. An overreaction he is likely to regret? Elif must have known what Zia was up to. From who else did he get the English formulations he needed? So, what follows from that?

Madeleine, apart from heaving deep sighs, was as silent now as before. I would have expected her to say something – if nothing else, something along the lines of so much wanting a chance to know Elif, to meet her sometime. I doubt they have even exchanged a single word with each other.

In five minutes, it was all over. Zia was back; his laboured breathing heard on the other side of the curtain.

Carlos may thank his lucky stars that Zia is a chain-smoker and not cut out for running, I thought, thankful, but not really cheered up.

"Come in," we called from inside.

Now we notice that he has been running in his stockinged feet and, furthermore, is leaving traces of blood. He lies down on the sofa and I examine his injuries while Madeleine fetches surgical spirit and the rest. He is lying with half-open mouth while I remove a piece of glass with a pair of tweezers, and more than usual, his teeth become visible, even the gap in his upper jaw, wider than I had realised. Yes, I would give him an implant, why not? Thinking about it, he wouldn't let me, would he?

35

Late afternoon, just to breathe deeply for a couple of minutes, I go out into the garden and look up the mountain, the left range, as most of the right is blocked by the cedar. So also this evening, and in fact I have performed this ritual several times, maybe in a subconscious attempt to conjure up Carlos from the darkness.

The moon is there, like a glimmering fig – as I have taken my glasses off – fixed on a dark blue carpet strewn with thousands of flashing *nar* kernels. The pomegranates are just about to ripen.

At midnight, Carlos comes back, the same way he left, and expresses no astonishment that we are still in the dining room, having moved to the big curved sofa.

"As far as I know, she is of legal age, certainly not responsible to that old relic, and I even less. He is rooted in the past, a leftover from the sultan era." Carlos says all this as if firing a delayed salvo in a still ongoing confrontation. Then, "I'm leaving. A car is picking me up at five thirty, to meet the bus to Izmir."

"In the morning?" Madeleine asks, between unhappiness and anxiety.

"Yes."

"And your breakfast?," she says awkwardly.

"The petrol station on the coast road, they have a bar."

Certainly not much of a breakfast there, we guess, but

Madeleine decides for both of us: "We will come with you to the petrol station."

There was no separate 'bar', only a corner in the shop with a few round café tables and tubular chairs which grated against the clinker floor when you moved them. Already someone sitting there, half-turned away from us, with something familiar about him – faded green jacket and white hair. Ah, not exactly a stranger, the Zoroastrian, although looking a little different now with a Greek philosopher's grey beard, tattered like an old nosebag. His eyes at half-mast, he was perhaps occupied with his prayers (many, many times a day according to Mr Hotty). To my surprise, Carlos gave him a small hand wave, which he wasn't likely to notice. Could he be a relation of Hotty, an uncle perhaps?

We had ample time, as the bus should show up around dawn. What the station attendant had to offer was slices of bread, cheese, sausage and marmalade, packaged in plastic cases and stored in a cooler between stacks of soda and screen-wash containers. Struggling with the packages, Madeleine and Carlos fixed them with their healthy bolt-cutter teeth while I went to borrow a chisel. It's not only my teeth; thumbs too.

"Carlos…" Madeleine said.

"Yes?"

He didn't look at all affected by what he had gone through, certainly not haggard or anything, rather the reverse, as if a bit more mature; well, poised is a better word.

Licking her lower lip, she looked him straight in the eye. This was a way of expression, as familiar to Carlos as to me, that appeared from time to time in some situations.

"As I have already told you, I am not quite without resources. You may ask your Monsignor whether he is willing to accept a donation instead of your voluntary work. And so, you can at least get rid of that."

Unaffected gratitude took possession of his face. Mine was probably expressing surprise, as I didn't know that Madeleine had finally come to terms with the idea that my assets should be divided equally between us. Or, as I also used to say: one-third each – Ivar, my helper, should have as much.

I had never been ready to support Carlos' ideas, since they failed to convince me. Also, there was his manner. He may have thought there was money for him in my tree of prosperity. Just needed a little shaking. Or more, that he was entitled to it? Was that what he had been thinking? And then, as he realised it was badly thought out, he took swings at me, all the harder, until he was blue in the face, never seen him that mad before or since.

We drank our plastic bottled water, which tasted just as it does when your brain is overflowing with desire for a cup of strong coffee. Wasn't even cool. Yet, coffee addiction may have been an even bigger problem for Carlos than for Madeleine and me.

He was drinking straight out of the bottle, anything but avidly, and holding it distractedly in his hand, he said: "Thank you, both of you.

"You see, this is the game. My agreement with Monsignor is there and can't be changed. A point of honour."

He added a confirmatory nod. Then, still with bottle in hand, he performed some shoulder rolls and the water followed his movements.

"Besides," he went on, "this liaison is a stepping stone to my next career – like I have told you, in Christian asset management. So, I need him for that too."

"Is that so?" said Madeleine – or was it me? I don't remember. "In what way? Is he an economist?"

"No, no. It's a matter of reputational management."

"Of what?"

"*Reputation management.*"

Vaguely, I remembered this expression from an FT article about a big bank in London that had got into a scrape. Yes, Barclays, it was called, caught with its fingers in a pot of profit from guidance on interest rates, doctored rates. A new boss was hired to polish up the brass plate: values and reputation! But, who knows, a bear hug from a high-profile cleric might have done the trick too.

"He is the moral guarantor behind the idea," Carlos added.

"Moral guarantor, is he now?" I rejoined without thinking twice – yes, this time, it was certainly me – perplexed with knobs on.

Quite often, I am a man of nimble wit, able to identify stupidity just a millisecond before it's slipping off, in contrast to those who need more time, not to mention all those who can't do it even then. Not now.

A moment's silence. He wasn't having it but didn't appear to have a reply ready.

At last he rose, but in so doing, he sent the chair backwards with a crashing squawk that made us grimace. The Zoroastrian, momentarily off Zoroastrian peacefulness, turned round to us with an angry look on his face, jerking his head quickly from side to side a couple of times like the woodpeckers in our cedar. Picking up his carry-on bag, Carlos headed for the lavatory. I never had the knack of detaining him in a discussion that wasn't to his liking.

Moral guarantor – gives you a lot to think about, no doubt. Is it that forgiveness has led to a business idea? If it's not the other way around: a business idea leading to forgiveness. Or is it all nothing but a business venture? If so, it mustn't be Pater Everyman to redeem him; it should be a *man of rank and mark,* Monsignor Piero. Those were the words used, were they not, when Carlos first told us about him?

Well, a young man went abroad, dipped a toe in something

toxic and became infected all over. I looked at Madeleine without being disposed to share my thoughts with her. And she looked at me, inquisitively. Neither of us in the mood to talk, it seemed.

A penny for Carlos' thoughts right now. I continue my meditations as he stands in front of the mirror; you could hear the buzzing from the electric razor. About his Pater, perchance? Or Zia? Was he reviving how he had contrived within a hair's breadth to come out of it all scot-free? Is it likely that Zia has said his last word yet?

His computer bag was left on the edge of the table, which yielded a little under the weight. Heaven knows what's on that hard drive. Anyway, better not to know.

Returning to us, Carlos was well shaven and smelled of cologne. He tucked in his chair almost inaudibly behind him.

"My major problem," he said, apparently picking up where he had left off, "is that Elif won't support me in it."

"In what?" asked Madeleine.

"My arrangement with the Monsignor."

"Really?"

"She isn't fond of my colleagues and our Egyptian counsel!"

"What do they have to do with your… stepping stone?"

"In the short run: nothing, almost nothing. Later, there will be a link."

"Elif doesn't trust them, does she?" I asked.

He gave no response.

Ignoring someone's question, as I understand it, is almost never an option, and if you don't want to give an answer, you should at least go to the trouble of wriggling out of it in a dignified manner. That's the rule – if not a moral rule, at least one of etiquette.

Actually, I had rather wanted to ask about Carlos and Elif, their relationship, but I wasn't sure this was the right time for that, nor the right place, either, and even so, it was probably off-limits for me.

"If Elif returns home, with no money and no job," said Madeleine, "she will be forced to live off her family. It's not hard to imagine how that will be for them. If she will be accepted at all, mind you. It's not as if we are in Stockholm or London.

"Not even Istanbul," she said at last after a pause and a sigh. "And it might be uncomfortable for us."

I was of course happy for such a declaration, and hoped it could not be read on my face.

"Why? You are not involved!" exclaimed Carlos.

Whether he didn't understand or didn't want to was impossible to guess.

I could have come up with something snarky: *Now, the money Madeleine just offered you can be put to good use here, a golden opportunity. Let's ask Zia's family how much they want in compensation for Elif's situation, such as it is or is soon to be, plus for retaining me as a friend.* Equally snarky, and true: *Zia told me what he would have told you, had you not cut and run: even the dogs will laugh at me!*

Much as I quivered on the inside, I confined myself to saying:

"You don't know how it works down here. Zia is not without social influence. He's a man people listen to."

There was a steady flow of machines pulling up at the petrol pumps now – many small pickups, including Kent Bread and the newspaper van, which were heading for the village and Liman – while we were waiting at our table without exchanging many words. The pump attendants in dark blue overalls, one at the beginning, four now, scurried back and forth between the vehicles, and at last the imposing Izmir double-decker arrived, dimming both the light from the leggy pylons out there and the dawn itself.

Carlos told us he would 'keep in touch' by email as usual. I heard myself saying: "If there is room on the bus, we can go with you. We haven't got much on today."

"Yes!" Madeleine agreed without the slightest hesitation.

He looked at us for a moment, without apparently finding anything out of the ordinary, and there was nothing to discover, either.

"Fine," he concluded.

Madeleine and I were sitting on the back seat; Carlos seated a few rows in front of us. Hesitantly, the morning sun was coming through the side windows. At Madeleine's temple, I saw some grey strands. Well, there is a first time for everything. Although not so surprising after all; she can't stay looking young all her life.

We looked at each other with surprise, both with a jumble inside, I should guess, perhaps one and the same confusion. What is the sense of sitting here? If to gain time, for what?

Is she also thinking about Carlos and the priest? That he is given a clean slate which he can then enter into his resume: *social responsibility, charity, critical mind;* something along those lines. I couldn't believe penitence could be used in that way, as a merit. Unless it wasn't the genuine article – but something else, posing?

"Madeleine," I say, "the *Moral Guarantor*... When you think of it."

Keenly awaiting the rest, she looked me in my eyes. But that was all, and Madeleine held her tongue.

With the risk that Carlos might hear us, it wasn't easy to confer freely; the engine was right beneath us and you had to raise your voice. "So let's creep down the toilet staircase." I giggled at the idea, loudly, it seemed, as Madeleine turned her head at it.

*

At Adnan Menderes Airport (named after a former prime minister, deposed by the military), there was no time for talking with each other, only for stress. Flushed, we reached the red rope barriers in front of security control. For some moments, we halted there, allowing others to pass, until Madeleine and I started moving with him a couple of stanchions on the other side of the rope.

Besides his neat barrel-bag, he had only the laptop to put on the scanner belt. His lips pucker into a smile of sorts and there is a nod too.

"I am so glad I came. Thank you, to both of you. My self-esteem has returned one hundred per cent."

36

We took a taxi to Izmir. While scouting for a place to live in Turkey, we had had our command post there, from which we made almost daily reconnoitres along the Mediterranean coast. Had the circumstances been different, our trip now might have been a nice sentimental journey. We were both sitting on the back seat, Madeleine looking out to the left, I to the right. A steady flow of vehicles and advertisement hoardings. Izmir is Turkey's third-largest city and it shows. My weary, yet tightly wound thoughts started goose-stepping like the Athens *Presidential Guard*; in other words, you couldn't take them seriously.

Suddenly I said:

"So, Carlos has recovered his self-esteem. That's probably what is needed in these modern times." I felt I should put in a modifier: *To make your mark, I mean.*

Without looking at me, Madeleine said, rather curtly: "Is that what is needed?" I had not anticipated that.

I asked the driver to take the route past the old *Elhamra Theatre*. Rather Turkish on the outside with blue ceramic glazes, its interior a miniature of the Paris Opera, where we once saw a performance of Donizetti's *Elixir of Love*. The house and the mise-en-scène were equally lovable; a wholly traditional presentation, so no dashes of polygamy or gayness, which might have been tempting for directors to play with in an opera like this.

Halfway there, we changed our minds and asked him to drop us off at the Clock Tower Square instead, for even more nostalgia.

Much to our liking, we found it still rather quiet, just a few people feeding the birds at one end, and young girls peddling wares at the other. We sat down on a bench in between, close to the Ottoman-era tower with the elegant fountains at its base. During the months we had spent in Izmir, police vans had taken up positions on the square, but for us it had been an abode of peace even then.

Some graceful Turkish doves were coming closer, peering at us. We had nothing to give them and, though a lover of birds, Madeleine started to seesaw a sandal-clad foot in their direction.

"When Carlos told us he had seen a priest," she said, "the very day he arrived, remember? – and that he would do penance within the church…"

She faltered and I nodded a couple of times while she seemed to be searching for words. "…I was flustered, of course, but I had no doubt he was serious about it. But little by little, I began to feel it was more for show."

Yea, so that the crooked will become straight and the rough ways smooth, I thought, but didn't say it because much as it would have been fun, Madeleine's dislike of Bible words, even if frivolously used, held me back.

It was the turn of the pig-tailed little girls to try their luck in front of us. As I had anticipated their visit and would not have liked our conversation to be disrupted, I gave them the two yellow lira coins I already held in my hand but accepted just one pack of paper handkerchiefs, their chief ware, since we only had Madeleine's little *kilim*-patterned bag for pills and toothbrushes to put it in. We got nice smiles when the transaction was completed, a matter of ten seconds at most.

So, I reflected, Madeleine shares my thoughts. That was what I had wanted, wasn't it? That we be as one again? But I certainly didn't want to see her heart sink.

"Showcase," I said. "Never tried to give your teacher a false impression?"

"Only about *trifles*," she snorted, "nothing comparable to this at all. For fear they would fail me."

"Me too, fearing they would lower my undeservedly high marks. Incidentally, I was good at it, or so I thought, which at that age comes to the same thing."

She snorted once more and restarted the seesawing. *Mark, I wanted to tell the pigeons, she isn't guilt-tripping you this time.*

"Trifles or not," I ventured, "does it really matter? Posing is as common as lying, don't you think, and the modern view is that lying is not always a bad thing."

"Of course it matters! Lying and posing, don't try to talk down bad things! It matters for himself! The forming of his own character!"

"Maybe he doesn't know it's posing? Or knows it fairly well but also knows what he's doing. I was posing throughout all my working life."

"You needn't grovel in the dust just to humour me."

"No trouble at all, really, happy to do it."

She didn't even snort. Stupid of me; it wasn't up to the mark.

In front of City Hall behind us, a gaggle of tourists was gathering with much arm-flapping among them and a good many selfie sticks popping up.

They would probably be hearing something about the history of the city: Smyrna of yore, pearl of the Ionian Federation, Homer's birthplace, under Turkish rule for 600 years. And of the clock tower, which they would soon come down to take a closer look at, and which incidentally is even more spectacular in the evenings when illuminated. Shameful as it was, I would rather not have them around us just now.

"We could go to Bird Paradise, Cenetti," I said, "either today or stay overnight and do it tomorrow."

Seeing no reaction, I continued:

"As is well known, the sight of five thousand *phlegmatic, flamboyant flamingoes* is equal to one hundred milligrams of vitamin C. Remember Linus Pauling and *Megadoses*? Just what we need!"

"Ascorbic acid? Your stomach couldn't stand that!"

"My wife's little rose-tummy does. And on top of this joyous proposal, she just got some damned smart alliteration. As a financial mogul in the *Financial Times* had it, that ain't hay."

She wouldn't give me credit for any of it.

"Where do you find the energy? You've had no more sleep than I have."

Ah, two blunders in a row, almost a record. After a moment's sullen silence, I said:

"We are both disappointed, angry even, and how could it—"

No chance she would hear me out.

"I am sad, and I pity him, too," she said in a harsh voice.

"In a way, shouldn't Elif also be pitied?"

She shook her head vaguely. Instead of staring at the paving stones, she now turned her eyes towards the clock tower, which was about to strike.

"As for disappointment," I said, "I feel disappointed with myself."

The eleven tinny chimes began to sound.

Funny how disturbed I was on hearing that Carlos had been seeking the church's blessings. Understanding now that it was just posing feels twice as unpalatable. You would have expected half as much.

We sat there until the gaggle started to trickle down to us – selfies, laughter, video cameras and all.

"Okay, let's go for Cenetti," Madeleine said, and we sought each other's hands.

37

When we got inside the gates, the first words Madeleine uttered were "I don't like this park at all," and she wrinkled the corners of her eyes. "What is it even called?"

We had passed a cage of lemurs, quite small animals with black and white rings along their tails, in a zoo housed at the edge of a larger park in the city centre, but when we reached an elephant enclosure housing two listless beasts she said that was enough for her.

"You liked it last time we were here," I said without thinking.

Dispiriting though this 'animal park' might have been, it was the hotel that haunted her. A four-star establishment with much to speak in its favour: excellent location in the heart of the city, well managed, restaurant, good enough or even more than that. The pianist had performed one old favourite after another –*As Time Goes By, Blue Moon*, along those lines – with a steady hand until some trickiness got in the way and he took to improvising or just skipped a few bars, all the time smiling good-naturedly. However, when it was time to settle down for the night, Madeleine realised that the only window could not be opened, and the lattice outside was not just an ornamental pattern but an encroachment on her sense of freedom.

Uncertain what to do, we sat down on a low wall shadowed by an inclining lotus tree with no zoo attraction in sight, our faces like people who had lost their way to somewhere.

Madeleine put her woven sunhat aside and lamented: "After all, we don't even know what Carlos wants, what he is after."

"Whether it's a quest for money, status, thrills or…"

"Yes."

To mollify, I said: "Who knows what people are after? There is also leading a good life, of course, driving ideas, and so on. Sometimes they may not even have sorted it out for themselves. Might even be a means to something else."

"So Carlos is motivated by *ideas?* Is that what you think?"

"Once in a while, yes. At other times, no."

Wasn't this the epitome of my own persona? Fluctuations like bond rates. If not worse. Had I ever set my heart on anything? Except furthering my career, which much to my surprise I finally became estranged from, turning into a longing for inner peace. Well, plus a dash of philanthropy – for reasons… for reasons of their own connected to my rehabilitation. Was I exaggerating? It didn't feel so.

"We know even less about Elif," I said.

"A minor problem, really," she replied, and then, in an enquiring sort of way, "she called you once to do her a favour, didn't she? Why would you respond to her?"

"I suppose, as I told you, there was no one else around."

"She was riding on your friendship with Zia."

"No, no." Almost immediately, I corrected myself: "Well, that's as may be. But it wasn't as if I was manipulated into helping her. I was certainly free to say no."

"Though you didn't."

"In the way of helpfulness, it was about the only thing I could come up with."

"Then it was because you wanted to say no, but couldn't?"

"Well, I don't know, maybe."

Lame answers, these; but I suppose I thought she was on

the wrong track. She had picked up a couple of the thin lotus twigs that had fallen from the wall and were almost stripped of their foliage, testing their flexibility. I guessed she was intent on mending the tear in her hat brim that she got from the traffic that morning.

Taking heart in the distractive power of braiding, I asked: "If we are responsible for Carlos, are we not also responsible for Elif?"

"That's for her family, not us."

On a bench a little way away, an elderly man with a cane and a cap, peaky blinder style, had been sitting for a nap, it seemed, and now a young mother sat down there too with her pram. He didn't look up. She unstrapped her toddler and started peeling fruit, but within minutes, he (or she) seemed to take a much stronger interest in us than in the presumably sour mandarin slices. Again and again, he inched forward towards us, big brown eyes, bushy black hair, and his mother pulled him back each time. I was grateful for that, as I was concentrating on our discussion and would rather not be bothered. In my prime, before my breakdown, I had been as sharp and multifunctional as a Swiss Army knife.

"Still, I could at least ask around," I said.

We were sitting idle and silent, a bit down in the dumps, it appeared, until I had another go: "What's its name, the place you are going to work in next week, the Grand Palace?"

"Why would she be much different than her sisters, if I may ask? Empty-headed, cat-walking," she exclaimed, with some extra wrinkles to the corner of her mouth added to those, rather few, she had had there since a few years back. I didn't remember Elif's sisters walking in any particular way at Zia's birthday party.

"She can manage correspondence and knows how to do bookkeeping. She can roll her eyes, too, when that's required," I added for the fun of it.

"If their relationship isn't right, what can we possibly do about it?"

"Carlos of course has his companions, and their ally, that Egyptian shipping person, and will land on his feet," I said. "It's different for her."

"No need to assume the worst."

"I don't. If she must return home, how will her family take it? Unmarried, not even engaged, a mistress and a maintenance burden to boot. Might well be rejected."

Embarrassing that I had to repeat this; I thought she was with me. Well, could be a temporary about-turn, and besides, I feared I wasn't much better myself.

"Anyway, Zia is a modern man," asserted Madeleine. "He has a wife without a veil who works as a hairdresser, right? And he loves new things…"

"Oh yes, spendthrift in that quarter he is. Incidentally, he is set on buying a veteran sports car, not cheap stuff. But family honour is a different kettle of fish. He's certainly no friend of frivolity spendthrift. Of a female or male kind; wouldn't make any difference. Anyway, the most important thing might not be how he sees it, but others' way of looking at it. His pride in his daughter is common knowledge, and relatives and friends share it – spendthrift-wise, so to speak," I added, hoping she would find me funny.

We were not very comfortable on the wall. To be sitting on rough limestone for a long time needs more '*sitting flesh*' than we are endowed with – a verbal atavism from my schooldays, my German teacher admonishing us at every turn: *Youngsters, grammar is nothing but Sitzenfleish*. We started to walk in the direction we thought the larger Cultural Park was, at least I in the hope of coming across an ice-cream stand. Otherwise, we might leave the area and look for a good café.

It didn't occur to us to shelve our discussion.

"Anyhow, we don't even know her, and so it would just look odd if we took any responsibility for her."

"Would it, really?"

"Besides, if she might need support sometime, just might, we shouldn't get involved. What would Carlos think? A charge against him for something, he may say."

I wasn't bent on accusing him of anything, or inflicting something on him. But I wanted to feel I could think freely and act freely. Carlos, I wanted to say, may herd the camels or leave the land – a saying I liked very much but seldom had a use for. Thank goodness I didn't.

"Only if he would take it as one," I said.

"What is the correct way of taking it then?" Madeleine asked.

At a stroke, my appetite for ice cream had changed, if not to say transfigured, into a desire of a far greater intensity for coffee – a double latte it ought to be; no, a triple.

"Let's go to the Hilton. Big hotels are always reliable, part of their business concept, don't you think?"

The most direct route proved to be the least pleasant to walk – narrow with a lot of traffic. A couple of times we changed sides, which didn't help much and was also a tricky thing to do. At one such running-the-gauntlet, Madeleine said:

"Remember, Carlos is a sensitive person."

All right, he is, I soliloquised, and so is Madeleine on his behalf. But likewise so am I – now that I have reached the stage in life when my dentist wants me to start with between-teeth brushes. Yes, sensitive, body and soul, with no less merit for special treatment than any other. Why don't we commission a construction engineer to make a parallellogram of forces or something to find out what our three sensitivity vectors sum up to? He would in good faith find that they cancel each other out.

These tumultuary reflections wouldn't do as an answer to Madeleine of course. Under stress, I can't give thoughtful answers, particularly not when walking in an exhaust gas ravine. I never know when it knocks on my door; it's according to an algorithm of its own. Like Google's, you are not supposed to know.

We found our way to a rather small terrace halfway up the building, which was probably not intended for temporary guests wandering about with large latte glasses in their hands. But with Turkish as a trump card – it's really to your credit if you try to speak the language, and I'm a talented trier – I meted out on my watch our promise to sit there just for a little while, and so we got the green light. Nice view over the Izmir bay, our lattes just perfect.

Half the glass gone, I felt composed enough to continue our discussion – or maybe debate would fit better. The terrace was empty save for two young women in a corner dressed in bright tunics.

"Madeleine, here is what I am thinking. Carlos understands his relationship with Elif as that between two companies. Like a merger. Just that at this moment, for the future, there is no deal! So no true merger, no hooks.

"A piece of cake. For him, that is. And Elif, if he goes down paths she doesn't really want to tread, what can she do? Return home? At least in my eyes, she will find herself much less able to look after her own interests, and would be well served with an alternative."

"We know very little about their relationship," said Madeleine, "just that they may disagree about the course, and you would like to have an input, to provide one of them with an *alternative*. And that would do it?"

"Yes."

I uttered it decisively, but sounded a full retreat a few seconds later: "No, not yes. Do what?"

"That's my question exactly. What do you want to achieve?"

I will lose this argument, I thought. Had my brain been a muscle, it would be bobbing in lactic acid by now.

"Fairness," I said. "Just *fairness*."

"Fairness? Accustomed as he is to getting his own way, I think it would be healthy for him to face a little opposition every now and then, but I still don't see what our involvement is going to achieve, besides self-satisfaction or something on your part."

"A certain amount of that. So be it," I said, with bad grace.

She had put it to me that I am an egocentric, or worse: egotist? I cupped my hand over my chin. Unshaven, although no worse than normal. Yet, a stranger might have thought me a hobo. Is that why those two are staring…? A friend of mine would see that I was weary, my feelings a little bruised, on the verge of sore.

"I suppose it's the same with fairness as with other beliefs about right and wrong," I dared to say, and suddenly, out of the blue, felt quite inspired:

"Everyday moral life hardly rests on solid foundations. It's a hodgepodge I should say; some ethical principles mixed with emotions and prejudice, misinformation, conscience, and let's not forget the mood of the day, and almost all of the time, self-interest on top, which permeates our doings like those newly detected particles, Higgs bosons or whatever, which dole out mass right and left."

"Okay, there might be something in that," she said, which was nice of her, but, after a moment, added, "perhaps." And then: "So, you have figured this out now, about fairness? Just waiting for a convenient principle to pop up into your top storey."

I had shot myself in the foot, and only had myself to blame for her sarcasm.

I felt sat upon and with a shake of my head produced a surly "No." This sullenness was still there while my self-exculpatory centre (if there is such a thing) started working on the quiet: I hadn't said that word, *convenient*, had I?

In the light blue sky over the Izmir bay a big orange bug was approaching us now, set to start descending, ear-splittingly, towards the landing pad on top of this giant shoebox. And so our coffee recess came to a natural end.

Our hotel wasn't more than a few blocks away. We decided to have a simple meal of eggplant *börek* before leaving, being the only ones apart from a few guests drinking beer. The pianist, dark suit and red tie, came up to us from nowhere to ask us: "What can I play for you?"

He was on the verge of adding *tonight* when I beat him to it: "*Für Elise*" just slipped out, together with a little giggle. As a little girl, Madeleine had quit piano, and now she shook her head vehemently, but the pianist gladly took the bait, and this sweet piece, of ill fame with many a baby boomer, he performed with bravura, first as it is conventionally played, then as a suite of improvised versions – jazz, blues, Arab (or Turkish?) folk melody and more – which lasted I don't know how long, half an hour maybe.

Formerly a piano teacher, he had been a jazz pianist too. He accepted our envelope with a smile, and swollen fingers that made us even more amazed at the ease of this playing.

Half an hour of joyful relaxation pure and simple this had been, my only rest from myself during the entire trip. I hoped it would stay that way, but it was not to be. I couldn't stop chewing along this mental chicklet which had lost its sweetness a long time ago.

Admitting my petty motives as I had, a case of fairness could still be made: helping to rectify warped circumstances. Right?

Just playing with an idea: could I have taken a different view? Elif had called me after Carlos' excoriation, which was a very gracious gesture that had gladdened my heart. Well, if she hadn't, would I have pursued her case equally as strongly?

If Carlos had never fired his salvos, what difference would that have made, if any? And if my mistake to use the phrase 'prodigal son' had never been made? And, the mother of all ifs: had I just vented my opinion differently, in a less disputatious, softer way, who knows if Madeleine wouldn't have sympathised more with my way of thinking, and taken a less dim view?

Evocative thoughts, no doubt. But counterfactuals are unreliable company. You never know where you might end up with them.

38

Returning from Izmir, a strange feeling, a vague doubt, came over me: how much longer were we going to have our place in Liman, in Turkey even? The logic behind it has slipped my mind and maybe I was just nudged by the fact that our Turkish odyssey had started out from Izmir, possibly some kind of inverted nostalgia.

What had attracted us most was the general calmness –not so much what was in front of us, the sea and the life there, nice and small-scale, or the flat stretch in between with its plant and animal life, as the mountain slopes and the hollow behind us where you would mostly meet with hikers from somewhere east or west, walking slowly with heavy feet. Or the camel and horse farm, gone now, just a quiet meadow, but which had been a picturesque contribution to the landscape. Camels are charming, tranquil creatures when treated well.

Not to mention the inherent safeness around here. There is little if any crime, and many doors are left unlocked even at night. True, we are not prepared for a tsunami if one comes. The giant waves would be cleaved by the *big cheese* but effortlessly united again, and then what? Zia shakes his head at this scenario; no one has ever brought it up, not to Abdullah's recollection, either.

Of course, we had hoped that all this would make for internal harmony: naively.

Whatever the reason, I came to reflect during the first post-Izmir week on how firmly we really were rooted to this place, whether it was unwise to change a winning horse, if winning it was, and where we might otherwise choose to live – not in Sweden, not until oblivion had made a final sweep of my mind, fatigue memories. Besides, it is illusory to believe that you can jump back into the slipstream of something that was left years ago, even if you wanted to.

Concurrently, I was trying to write a talk about the dangers of skin-lightening, which I had promised without any real enthusiasm to give in London. I have been able to keep my low BMI over the years, partly thanks to stress, but the same cannot be said for my *regret ratio*.

I had just reached the sections about bans on skin lightening products when the landline in the kitchen rang. Less used than our mobile phones, its signal is better, and Jens gives me a *general report* on this line about every other week, although I have told him he is always free to act in the way he thinks best, so de facto it's for his sake rather than mine. Now he had already called twice in the last month, but Fatosh can often use it when on a shopping spree somewhere, and Zia too, for that matter, if a lot of mail or an urgent letter is waiting for us.

I couldn't hear Madeleine moving and so I went downstairs to answer it.

"Hello, Dr Edman, it's Elif Gülen, Zia's daughter, if you remember?"

"Oh hallo. Hallo, Elif," I repeated a snap louder for Madeleine to hear, or perhaps just out of perplexity.

"Am I calling at a bad time?"

"No, no, not at all."

There were chaotic hissings from my mental prompt box: whatever this is about, do not promise anything; silence is golden, sleep on it.

Lips firmly squeezed together, Madeleine peered in from the hall, like when, long ago now, Elif called me after Carlos had entertained me with his indignant fuming in return for my saving him and his buddies from an embarrassing mess.

And like last time, I wasn't sure what to make of it. I wouldn't believe she thought me flattered, or impressionable or something. Well, maybe impressionable.

It was just a short call. Elif will be in Ankara for a couple of days together with her younger sisters, I explained to Madeleine.

"And you promised to see her?"

"Well, yes, as it happens, I did. Because I thought it a good opportunity to talk to her."

"Why does she want to meet you? She just called you without any reason?"

"No, no. She wanted to talk to me – just a thought, she said, since she happened to be close by, sort of."

She sniffed at this. "Why doesn't she come here?"

"Something related to her sisters," I guessed. "Maybe also she doesn't want to see her family right now."

She drew in air, paused, and let it out, noisily, the way she teaches people.

"That's you in a nutshell, Birger: your hidden talent, anything simple, made complicated in two seconds."

To maintain my dignity, I said: "It's my prerogative to say that."

39

"If you feel tempted to bring up the idea of an alternative job, what will Carlos' reaction be, do you think?"

I thought we were done with this.

Who knows how he will react? Given what I learned when he fired his *Stalin Organ*, he is certainly capable of behaving nastily, and I don't know what mood he is in. Something may well snap inside him. This I could have said, but didn't.

"Nothing negative, I hope, since this is not about him, it's about Elif."

"So you think we should feel more solidarity with Elif than with Carlos?"

There was something strange about this question, but I couldn't put my finger on it at first.

Although we were sitting in Mr Hotty's arbour (or rather, that he calls his arbour), there were people around us – some wearing work pants with tool-pockets, to do with the relay station on the mountaintop presumably – you could almost hear the silence falling between us.

I took a big gulp from my straw-coloured Efes, lovely, cold, if teeth-tingling, stroked my chin a couple of times – and then I had it.

"I don't know that solidarity for her is due, but then fairness, which this is about, doesn't need that footing."

"What does it need, then, according to you?"

"Well, just a moral feeling."

"But you don't think much of that, a *hodgepodge*, you said."

Trapped! At least there was nothing malicious in her face, a rather ordinary fifty-five-year-old face, unusually young-looking perhaps, with stringy hair, since she hadn't washed it after her swim.

A pack of dogs had come to visit us and they know how to behave, lying still on the sand, not too close, hoping. I can't see Sabhia among them.

"As you can imagine, I wonder what you are going to offer Elif."

"Haven't given it much thought, actually. I suppose I will refer her to Jens."

"Isn't that rather dodgy, playing down your own role?"

I wasn't prepared for this discussion. I had been about to visit the greenhouses after a quick lunch, but now there was an obvious question to be asked:

"If I call Jens, would you approve of that?"

To think it over, she put a thumb over her upper lip, on the place where young people like to implant a stud (the medusa piercing place). Pushing it up so that the tip of her incisors showed, she let slip a vague sound, a drawn-out umm, and this was the tone on which our discussion closed.

Had we been alone, I might have leaned across the table, sealing it with a kiss on her forehead.

We heard shooting in the mountains, impossible to say from what direction. Earlier that day, a company of hunters had passed us with guns and grunt tubes. The wild boars have been pests this year, as they always are when they are short of food. With perked-up ears, the three technicians turn their heads towards the west, perhaps hoping to get something for their freezers.

Not just shooting, but a sputtering noise could be heard, like a malfunctioning exhaust pipe. Probably Zia, I guessed, collecting extra provisions for dinner. Zia still nods but avoids patting my back. True, he is not fully certified for Western living, but he is my friend and has many good qualities –considerate, grateful, humorous… loyal, yes, that too. Can I get back what was there before? I will have to wait and see. Or do something drastic, like buy him a Lotus. *Lotus Ivory*, wasn't it? Then Madeleine, perhaps: So, reconciliation is something money *can* buy, one million lira, is that what you are saying? Yep, that's where even the prices in *How to Spend It* fall short. Joking apart, is it really that bad a thought? It's his dream and this is the only way it could ever come true – and likely to calm things down with kith and kin, and impress them greatly.

*

"If I come up with an idea myself, would you dismiss it out of hand?"
There was a short silence.
"I can't bear to talk about this any longer. I'm fed up with it."
"Me too, if that's any consolation."
"I can't tell you until it's done."

*

A few days later, it was hatched.
Elif's job would be to develop a long-term charity function, I told Madeleine. She would initiate projects, take care of all the begging letters and manage contacts with the Ivar Foundation. If this wasn't a full-time occupation, Jens could fix that with support tasks for her in his office. Anyhow, she could have her desk with his in there.

"Have you done any risk analysis?" Madeleine asked.
"What do you mean by that?"
"You should know, since you asked Carlos that."
"I don't know whether it applies here," I said meekly.

40

Elif had asked me if by any chance I was going to visit Ankara. When we did the Kash rescue operation together, I probably told her that I was wont to do so at least twice a year. She planned to meet her sisters there, and could adapt to my schedule, since she was 'anxious to talk to me'. We ignored my trip for a while, Madeleine and I, a disturbing comfort, but the closer to the departure date, the more the silenced questions clamoured for attention. The day before (or was it days before?) she asked:

"Have you spoken to him yet?" She meant Jens.

"There's no need."

"No need?"

"He will do what I ask him. I'm the founder."

"You didn't sing that song when you told me about your money, that Carlos couldn't have any, that Jens decides, that everything is in his hands."

I shrugged – or perhaps I did nothing with my shoulders, just an awkward movement with my mouth.

"And how are you going to inform Carlos?"

My astonishment seemed to surprise her. Rightly so, perhaps, but it was genuine.

"So it's going to be behind his back?"

Why not? I thought, but gave it a thumbs-down in a flash.

"Well, it's only natural that Elif should do it."

Not in the best position to talk to him, I feared that anything I might say would be seen as stoking mischief. Why would I expose myself to the risk of being singed once more?

"A stab in the back," she said laconically.

I took a short pause for reflection, but would have been better off with a longer one.

"By the way," I ventured, "who knows what this means for Carlos? Crassly speaking, it might even be helping him out of a scrape."

"Helping him to dump her?"

I nodded.

"But in that case..." she said, making a sour face, "then what about *fairness* and the notion of *helping* her?"

"It's up to her to take her chance or not."

"Okay, say Carlos is told, and so gets an excuse to get rid of her. That's the logic, right? Then you help *him* and not *her*."

"Well," I said, with my tail between my legs, "just speculating."

Not exactly pleased with myself, I should have rewound, but feared it wouldn't go well. Perhaps I should have been a doctor of sophism instead of medicine. I wonder whether I haven't got a genius for it.

During my medical studies, we would video meetings with patients to improve our consultation skills. It is a useful technique but stressful; it can sometimes be rather disheartening to see yourself on screen. Recording my behaviour in private conversations –would that have been useful too? For enhancing some human qualities. Thank God it never happened.

We seldom keep each other company if it is only one of us who is about to leave, but we were now both standing there anyway, waiting for the taxi, at the usual place, and on the unspoken premise that perhaps not everything had yet been said.

There was a garbage smell, but not too bad, as it was still

early in the morning. Two cats that had mysteriously climbed on top of a squash-like rubbish bin with its lid only half-closed were now at a loss, as their claws did not grip on the tin plate.

"Birger, I agree that Carlos can be a complicated person at times, but perhaps it might be wiser to tackle this in another way. Is it really the right thing to do?"

"To my mind, it's the *best* thing to do," I said, and nearly continued: *if, for once, I feel something is the right thing to do, why shouldn't I do it?*

A stripy cat jumped off the rubbish tombola and started winding between Madeleine's bare legs, looking up at her, perhaps asking to be taken home, or for her help. When she backed away, it came over to me.

"You are a very sensitive person…"

"If you say so. Sorry, just joking."

"Birger, there is always a risk that you will feel bad about it if you follow your idea through," *don't you think?* her gloomy look seemed to add.

So, all of this boils down to a guilty conscience: Mine! Not to the one Carlos ought to have. If this is the argument of last resort, I will fight it down!

"A guilty conscience," I said, "that's certainly not a moral argument," intimating this was a glaring weakness.

"Neither is your *swap idea*."

"Swap? What swap?"

"Doing good to a girl now because you failed to do so in your youth. Anne, or whatever her name was."

These were not my words, no doubt about that, but I kept my counsel. By the way, my *bad conscience* no doubt suggests a blemish, my doing harm, so it is a moral argument after all. No, I can't accept it. I may be soft on willpower but on morals? Do I see myself as someone with low moral values? A wave of uneasiness hit me.

In this disheartened state, I got into the taxi –incidentally driven by same man who had taken us to Kash and shown us the play of colour on the water, Deniz by name – yet cheerily waving farewell, at least trying to.

In his amiable way, he tried to converse with me, which proved an unrewarding task: "So, you are going abroad?" No, to Ankara. "Ah, for business, I suppose," he ventured, turning this good-natured face towards me.

No, just to meet someone. He may have thought me queer fish, perhaps not the only one to think so.

41

Enmeshed in different threads of thought, but still in a similar mood, I called Madeleine in the evening and told her I would be delayed. Maybe I gave a sigh too, as I was still lying on the hotel bed after a round with my *trident relaxor* – a sturdy olive-picker in polished steel with sharp points to let loose on my skull; and indeed easily mistaken for some kind of medical utensil. Whether its effects are real or imagined, I can't say, and it is of no significance, of course. Come to think of it, Madeleine was very careful that Carlos should not see it in action.

"Where are you staying?"

"Usual place."

The Sheraton is designed as a lighthouse, but some people tongue in cheek say it was meant to be a wine bottle. This time, my room was about level with the etiquette, with a view which is unremarkable. However, there are fairly green surroundings, and through the window I could see blue birds with rusty breasts filling the air, barn swallows no doubt; who wouldn't want to be like those graceful creatures, sailing around so effortlessly? Then there is the coffee and the proximity to a first-class bookshop.

"What's the weather like?"

"The weather? Quite frankly, there is none!" In my youth, she might have sniggered at this. "Well, at any rate, it's a bit drizzling."

"How did it go?"

"…I didn't put forward my idea. We were discussing other things and her little sisters came along, which ended it, so we will continue tomorrow."

"Aha."

"Putting two and two together, their relationship isn't among the happiest," I said, "although Elif looks all right, young and healthy."

"How is she dressed?"

"Dressed? Well, trousers and sports shoes, those with a V-shaped logo. Adidas, perhaps? Cooler here of course," I added before coming to the point. "Anyway, she is pregnant. But they can't agree on what to do. Whereas she doesn't want to keep the baby, Carlos does. Surprising, eh?"

"Why doesn't she?"

"For one thing, it is far too early, she says."

"And for another?"

"No idea. Great expectations plunging into the Valley of Darkness perhaps?"

Madeleine would say this proves her point – we should sit on our hands – but she was silent. As quiet as the pair of swallows now pausing on the window ledge.

"Anyway, she wants to talk to someone about abortion, which can't be her mother, Zia even less; in fact, no relative, blood or otherwise, besides a cousin living in Honolulu."

We were silent for quite a while. This isn't so easy over the phone but it helps if you have been married for twenty-odd years.

"Now what?"

"I feel like throwing my idea in the trash. As for the rest… I really don't know how to *instigorate*."

This word, or non-word, was well known to her, as it was from *Winnie-the-Pooh*, which Madeleine had read to me to help me get to sleep during my burnout days. We use it a lot.

At length, Madeleine said in a calm and steady voice, normally modulated and with no doubt in it whatsoever, much like her working voice, I imagine:

"Birger, you can tell her that we will help her to find a solution."

"Are you serious?"

"Yes. I can join you now if you like. And once that is settled, we can talk to her about whether she wants another job."

Oh thou sweet cup.

She would reasonably bear the brunt of Carlos' reaction. As simple as that. I thanked her, thanked her again, eager to end the call quickly to get Elif's approval. Hopefully, Madeleine could catch an early flight.

Sweet cup given to me.

All done and dusted, I would scurry to the patisserie beyond the bookshop, the one with retro coffee cups in the window, and order two strong cappuccinos in a row. With a Viennese pastry. Later, a concert, anywhere. Something by Bach, or Mozart's *Requiem*, or an opera… who knows? Even jazz would be fine. Tonight, I will sleep like the king of the sloths.